VALKYRIE CONDEMNED

A LEGACY WORLD NOVEL

VALKYRIES RISING
BOOK 6

ALLYSON LINDT

ACELETTE PRESS

This book is a work of fiction.

While reference might be made to actual historical events or existing locations, the names, characters, places, and incidents are either the product of the author's imagination or are used fictitiously, and any resemblance to actual persons, living or dead, business establishments, events, or locales is entirely coincidental.

Manufactured in the United States of America

*To all my fellow Valkyries… My author friends… The women who made this entire thing possible… Thank you :**

PROLOGUE - MIA

WHOEVER THE SADIST WAS WHO INVENTED 6 A.M. lessons should be forced to attend them for the rest of their lives.

Then again, they might like that.

I'd have to think a little harder on the appropriate punishment.

I suppressed my yawn as the small group of adults I was teaching to read gathered their belongings. Most of them would go straight from here to their jobs, and were laden with whatever they needed to make it through their workdays.

The literacy class had been held at the library for years, and when I took over, there were never more than one or two people there. In talking to people, I'd realized it was because the classes started at four, so the library could close their doors at five thirty, and a number of the people the program was meant for were still at work at that time.

So I'd moved things to a corner of my comic book shop, and held lessons early in the morning once or twice a week. I still couldn't account for everyone's schedule, but it was a start. Some of them grabbed an extra cup of coffee and a bagel for their commute, and within a few minutes, the room was quiet again.

One of the faces I expected to see here today hadn't shown, and I was worried about her. As I folded chairs and stacked them in a corner, I wondered if I should call someone. She could be fine. She really didn't need the lessons anymore, given that last week she'd stayed late to discuss the finer details of *1984* with me.

And I didn't know who I would call anyway. The police? *Hey, one of my adult literacy students didn't come to class. No, I don't know where she lives. Or her last name. Or her first name…* She'd told me she was Sally one week. Then the next week it was Mary. When I asked her about the different names, she stammered and insisted one was a first name and one was a middle name.

I suspected she'd escaped a bad life, based on some of the little things she said and the way she was always looking over her shoulder.

I couldn't say I understood completely—my father was kind and loving. As I got older, I started to look more like my mother who passed away when I was a baby. There was a sadness in his gaze when he looked at me and thought I wasn't looking back.

He was always doting on me though.

The world he raised me in, on the other hand, had a lot more danger lurking around dark corners than it appeared on the surface. And some of the company that he kept, that he required me to keep… it hadn't been the worst, but it had sure wreaked havoc on my psyche.

"I'll take those." Caleb, the man who rented my extra room from me, grabbed three chairs from me, hefting them as if they were pieces of paper, and carried them to stack with the rest.

He looked slender, a couple inches shorter than my five-foot-eleven, but the dude was secretly jacked. He tried to hide it under looser clothing, but when he did things like maneuvering heavy folding tables with zero effort, it was clear he was more than the geeky persona he tucked behind glasses and faded T-shirts from thrift stores.

"Nice of you to show up, finally." I teased and started boxing up the bagels.

He snagged one, smeared half with cream cheese, and shoved half of that into his mouth in a single bite. The wiggle of his eyebrows and his shrug helped me figure out his muffled reply. "Just here for the food."

It wasn't true. He'd be here regardless. He and I met when I was still volunteering to do this at the library. He volunteered for the church down the street to teach English as a second language to immigrants. According to him, he had the gift of tongues.

Otherwise known as he was really good at picking up any language.

My phone chimed, and my best friend Scarlett's face appeared on screen. Lucky bitch had moved to Greece to run a hotel, and it was afternoon for her.

"Hey, bitch." I cradled the phone between my shoulder and ear, so I could keep working while I talked to her.

Caleb pointed to another door silently, and mimed carrying the tables into the storage room.

I gave him a grateful smile, both for the work and that he was giving me a little bit of privacy for my call.

"Morning, skank." Scarlett's greeting was bright. "Class is over, right? Can you talk? I need to tell you something." She sounded excited.

Which made me excited. "Ooh, secrets. This sounds like the kind of secret I'm going to like."

"You're going to *love* this. Seriously, you're going to shit yourself when you hear it."

That was a pretty impressive promise. My shop door swung open and I turned, surprised I still had students here.

The man who stalked in wasn't one of my students.

"I'll call you back," I said to Scarlett. "We open at ten," I called out.

When he turned toward me, his eyes narrowed. He strode across the room. "Where's Gretchen?" He stopped inches from me, and towered over me.

If he was looking to intimidate me, fuck him. I'd grown up around bruisers, and learned a long time ago that bullies weren't worth cowering to. "I don't know who that is." I held his gaze in an unwavering stare.

"Fuck you, you don't. She comes in here every fucking week. I've been watching."

Watching. Fuck. Did he mean Mary-Sally? "Then you know there's no one who comes here by that name."

"She didn't show today." He clenched a fist. "Tell me where she is."

I straightened to my full height, which still made him a couple of inches taller than me. "I don't. Know who. You're talking about." I spoke the words slowly and deliberately, to make my point.

He stepped closer, and I flinched on instinct. Damn it, I didn't want him to see that.

"You talk to her every week. You mean to tell me you don't know how to find her? You're one of those whores who's helping her hide." His breath was sour, like coffee, syrup, and alcohol.

When a bit of spittle hit my face, I was impressed with myself for not flinching this time. "I can't help you. You need to leave."

"Not until I have answers."

Though bullies weren't worth the effort, they were also difficult to make go away. My heart slammed against my ribs as he stood toe-to-toe with me. This wasn't all fear that pounded in my veins, though, and my hands curled into tight fists.

If I continued to stare him down, would he hit me? Had he hit Mary-Sally?

Because I would hit back.

Most days I wished I could be completely noble and passive, like Professor X in the beloved *X-men* comics that sat on my store shelves.

Moments like right now, I was more like Magneto. Willing to inflict a kind of permanent harm on those who dared to pick on the wrong people.

Fortunately—or maybe not—I had enough sense to know that may not go my way for a number of reasons. For instance, I knew how to throw a punch, I'd spent hundreds of hours dealing my frustrations to a large bag that hung in the gym in my father's building, but I wasn't good for much more in a fight.

And I'd rather not bruise my knuckles on this asshole. "Leave, or I'll call the police."

He wrapped a hand around my throat before I could blink, and shoved me into a nearby wall. "Where's Gretchen?" He squeezed, pressing his thumb into my windpipe and putting his face less than an inch from mine.

He was too close for me to swing with any effectiveness.

Panic set in as darkness licked at the edges of my vision. There were ways out of this. I knew there were. Why couldn't I think of them? Why didn't—

The man grunted and stumbled, his grip on me loosening.

I scrambled away, to find Caleb behind him.

Caleb threw a sharp, quick kick at the back of the man's knee, sending him tripping forward now that I was out of the way.

But this Caleb had shed the glasses, and stood in a stance with his fists raised, as he bounced on the balls of his toes. "You were asked to leave." His voice was cool. Icy, even.

Mr. Bully whirled and swung at Caleb with a punch so wide and obvious he could've sent a telegraph.

Caleb stepped aside, like we were in a fucking action movie, grabbed Mr. Bully's hand, and swung behind him with the man's entire arm.

I heard the distinct crack of a bone, and the man roared in pain.

Caleb didn't flinch. Instead, he pressed his face next to Mr. Bully's from behind. "Get. Out." Caleb's voice was pure threat. He didn't wait for a reply, and instead manhandled Mr. Bully to the front door, shoved him out, and locked the door behind him.

Oh, fuck me.

"Are you all right?" Caleb was back by my side, barely touching my neck.

I fingered the tender spots along my skin and swallowed back the tears that stung my throat and the insides of my eyelids. Because no matter what, no one got to see me cry in frustration. Caleb was nice enough, in fact I liked him more than I did most people. On late nights when I was alone and let my defenses down, sometimes I pretended he was as attracted to me as I was to him—I fantasized about all the sexy fucking things we'd do if that were the case.

But it wasn't, and men I crushed on didn't get to see me break down in moments of weakness, because I couldn't take care of myself against an imposing dickwad who thought demanding things got him what he wanted.

"I'm fine, thank you." My voice, my reply, were clear, and my tone too bright.

He studied me, his brow furrowed, then gave a brief shake of his head. "Good." We finished cleaning up, and got ready for the work day to start.

I called the police and gave them a full report, as well as all the information I had about *Gretchen*. They said they'd have someone swing by occasionally to check on me, and they'd keep an eye out for the man, but without more information, they couldn't do much.

Caleb wanted to stay and keep me company—keep me safe—but I couldn't intrude on his day like that, and I made him get back to his own schedule.

I managed to put the incident out of my head as

the hours ticked away, though after we opened, each time someone came into the shop, my nerves twitched. And my gut clenched.

By the time lunch rolled around, I desperately needed a break, or I was going to scream. At myself. For not being able to get over this.

Teddy, the guy who worked midday shifts showed up, and I took the opportunity to head into the back and get some air and clear my head. Also, to shove some food into my face.

Chips and soda made a lot of things better, especially when paired with cookies.

While I was eating, Scarlett called.

"Shit, I'm so sorry," I answered immediately. How did I forget to call her back?

"No worries. Is everything all right?"

No. But that was mostly because I couldn't do things like defend myself or the people who needed it. "Yeah. Totally fine."

"You're lying."

Busted. "It's not a big deal, really. Nothing new. You had news for me?"

"Not until you tell me you're all right and mean it."

Damn friends, always being concerned. "I'll be okay." This time I managed the reply with more calmness. "I'll be better if you tell me your awesome news."

There was a pause. She was thinking about arguing. "Fine. But only because this really will make you feel better. Magic is real."

My brain froze, half of it choked on a laugh and the other half glitching on *of course it is*.

Of course it *wasn't*. What was wrong with me? "Is this like you found the perfect, magical pair of shoes on sale?"

"No." Scarlett huffed. "This is like Panos is a god —as in *the* Panos, that guy I was telling you about who I thought was his lover, Arnlaug, is a berserker, and this woman named Kirby turned me into a Valkyrie."

Was she telling me about a new book she was working on? "I don't get it."

"Get what? What's there to get?"

"I'm looking for the punchline." Except that I knew Scarlett wasn't the kind of person who pulled pranks. That wasn't her. So what was the deal?

"There's no punchline. I'm serious." She sounded sincere.

And half of my brain still believed her.

Because I was delusional and hurt after this morning's encounter, and would cling to anything that made my fantasies more real.

She's not lying.

She was, though. For whatever reason. "Why did you really call?"

"Mia, I'm being serious. She gave me fucking wings."

Wings. Like Dark Phoenix.

I'd always wanted wings. And magic. Valkyries could fight, couldn't they?

Damn it.

I wasn't insane, though. And I wasn't in the mood for whatever this was. "I have to go. Congrats on the idea for your next book." That was what this was. She was telling me her next book was ready for me to give it an early read. "If you want a beta reader, send it over."

"Mia—"

"Bye." I disconnected before my brain could convince me she was right.

What if she is?

She wasn't talking about reality, because I wasn't insane, and magic only existed in fiction.

"Hey," Teddy poked his head into the break room. "Since we're kind of slow right now, do you want me to go pick up the mail when you're done with lunch?"

We had a lot of our mail go to a local paid mailbox place, and Teddy used *picking up the mail* as a daily excuse to take a vape break.

Not that I had a problem with that. "I'm done now, if you want to go."

"Thanks." He grinned.

I followed him back into the main room of the shop, and took my place behind the counter. Normally I'd straighten the place up to occupy my mind, or stock shelves, or something.

I'd already done that this morning to keep myself from thinking about the horrible encounter with Mr. Bully.

As if summoned by my thoughts, he walked into the shop.

Shit.

I reached for my phone, and it wasn't there. I must've left it in back after talking to Scarlett.

Double shit.

I grabbed for the cordless phone we used for the shop instead. There was pride and then there was stupidity, and I wasn't dumb enough to try to handle this guy without police help. Why didn't I call them this morning after he left?

He reached the counter before I did, and yanked the phone cord from the wall. Why, oh why, did I skimp on putting a panic button for my alarm system closer to me?

But this time I had the counter between me and him, and I wasn't above hitting him with anything in my shop, to get him to go away.

I wielded the phone like a club. A very small club. "Nothing has changed since this morning. Get out."

"Except that your boyfriend broke my fucking finger." Mr. Bully held up his right hand, to reveal a splint on his pinky. "So I'm going to break something of his."

I was pretty sure he meant me, and arguing any of the inaccuracies of his assumption wouldn't do me any good. I also refused to flinch like I had earlier. "How about instead, you turn around and walk out, or I'll break a more vital finger."

His snort-laugh sent ice spilling through me.

Why wasn't Caleb here? Or—*God*—Thac. My father's enforcer would make this man wish he'd never even thought about hurting another human being.

And why couldn't I take care of this myself?

Mr. Bully came around the counter, and I realized the horrible folly of my assumption that I was safe back here. The U-shaped space meant I was trapped now, between him and a lot of glass.

I pulled back the phone, ready to beat him as much as I could.

Scarlett appeared in the main floor space. *Blink*, she was here, with a man who had short horns barely peeking out from under his thick curls of hair.

Scarlett looked at me, then at Mr. Bully, who spun toward her. "Where the fuck did you come from?" he demanded.

"Greece," the man with Scarlett said.

"Fuck off." Mr. Bully lunged for me, but Scarlett was inhumanly fast. She and her companion moved with a blurred speed that made Caleb's actions this morning look absolutely sluggish. No matter where my attacker turned, Scarlett was faster.

I'd never seen her move like this. She was a normal person, like me.

And seconds later, her companion had Mr. Bully pinned to the wall by the door. Scarlett rested a hand on Mr. Bully's arm. "Don't come back here." When she spoke, there was a weight to her words. "Don't come near Mia. Don't go near anyone she knows. Pan can find you, wherever you are."

Though she wasn't talking to me, her voice made me feel like someone walked over my grave.

Mr. Bully's anger was gone, replaced with a vivid terror flashing in his eyes. He nodded, and walked out of the shop as quickly as he could.

"What did you do?" I had no idea which question to start with, so I grabbed one as dozens spilled in my head.

"I put the fear of death in him," Scarlett said.

"Pan?" I looked at her companion. "What are you both doing here? Did you fly in last night? Why didn't you tell me when you called me? Is this a joke after all?"

Scarlett strode toward me. "Not a joke. I came to prove to you I was telling the truth. This is Pan. Pan, this is Mia."

"Pleasure." He gave a short bow.

He was handsome. Almost pretty. No wonder Scarlett liked him.

"We arrived just now," Scarlett said. "He's how I got here. He can teleport from one place to another in a blink. It's one of his powers as a god."

The strength sapped from me, and I leaned against the wall for support. "What?"

"Like I told you on the phone." The air around Scarlett shimmered, and gorgeous wings appeared from thin air, sprouting from her back. "I'm a Valkyrie."

You can't be. He can't be a god. The protest died in my throat. I was looking at how very real her words were, and the longer I stared, the easier they were to believe.

It was like a veil fell away. Like a huge secret, something I'd known my entire life but had been too indoctrinated to acknowledge, was finally okay to think about. To talk about.

"Oh my *God*. You. Look. Incredible." I pulled her into a tight hug. "Holy shit. This is amazing." I should still be in shock. Still be filled with disbelief.

But I wasn't. Her news felt right. The proof was directly in front of me.

Scarlett grinned and twirled, showing off the new look.

Pan watched her every move with a kind of adoration I could only dream about someone watching me with.

"I need to know everything you can tell me," I said. "Start at the beginning and don't leave any of it out."

"I don't know much yet, but I'll tell you what I do," Scarlett said.

I grabbed chairs for both of them, and listened as Scarlett told me the story of meeting Kirby, and Pan filled in a couple of blanks.

They told me about Nyx, who was an ancient being who recognized Scarlett's potential and sent her to Pan, to keep her safe. About Pan's—Berserker—former lover who came to get Scarlett for his master but ended up falling for her, and then how this woman named Kirby showed up and gave Scarlett wings.

It was an amazing tale. Better than any comic, because it was real.

A tiny, nagging voice in the back of my head asked why Scarlett had this, and I didn't. Wanted to know why I still couldn't protect myself and others, the way I'd always wanted to.

I squashed that whiny little bitch of jealousy with a giant fist of happiness for Scarlett. I smothered the intrusive thoughts under a blanket of *holy shit, magic is real*. Because if there was a world where gods could blink from one continent to another, and women could make others ultra-powerful with a touch, then suddenly so much was right with my reality.

Magic was fucking real.

ONE
MIA

Protecting those who fear them.

The slogan on the cover of the X-men comic I was putting on the shelf taunted me.

It was a clever phrase. Catchy. Memorable. The kind of thing that made the brilliantly unique feel like they belonged.

Why would they want that? Everybody needed a place to belong. My mother passed away when I was a baby, and I didn't remember her. Despite my father doing everything he could to raise me with love in his world, I still felt most of the time like I wasn't in the right place for me.

So I got it.

What I didn't understand in the X-men comics was that so many of them wanted to be average—to blend in with the crowd and be like the rest of them.

If I could grow wings like Dark Phoenix, like Scarlett, I'd want to spread them and fly all the time.

"Phoenix Force, Phoenix Force, take me away." I muttered the mutated phrase from Labyrinth to the entire slew of absolutely no one in my comic -book shop and grabbed a statuette from the box on the floor. The beautiful figurine stared back at me with dark eyes, red hair like flames, and a body that could stop traffic —because she was curvy and sexy, not because she was thick.

And those fiery -red, orange, and yellow wings…

I put the Dark Phoenix collectible on the wire-frame shelf, next to the *Dark Phoenix Saga* limited-edition graphic novel, made sure both were straight, and returned to the register by the front door.

I needed to get over this mood. I also needed to lock up my shop, *Chapel Comics,* in a few minutes. The latter seemed far more likely to happen anytime soon.

Busying myself with closing tasks near the register was easy. I had this routine down after owning the shop for nearly ten years. The figure wasn't part of said routine, it hadn't needed to go on the shelf *now,* but when I saw Phoenix was in my late-in-the-day delivery, I had to put her on display.

Now I could go back to wiping down the counters that greeted customers when they walked in. My shop was in an old church, with stained -glass windows on all the walls, so no matter the time of day

—as long as it *was* day—muted, colorful sunlight streamed into my sales floor.

It was not only gorgeous to look at, but also highlighted the collection of limited-edition books that sat under the glass.

I finished the clean-up and gave another glance to the new Dark Phoenix display. Battling bad guys, good always coming out triumphant, it was a nice story and one I believed so desperately when I was a kid, but it wasn't reality.

Instead, the real world was the one I discovered when I was in my early teens. The world where my father had been hiding the fact that he was a powerful crime boss. That he was the law in our neighborhood, and that the same money that had spoiled me as a child ensured that so many others suffered.

That wasn't the hard lesson, though. The nuance, that massive gray area that lay between *good* and *bad,* that I'd learned to see and understand, was the rough thing for me to accept.

Sometimes Magneto was right—humanity could be the biggest monster.

At least superheroes were real. Not like in the comics, and not that I got to be one of them, but Scarlett was a Valkyrie. A fucking badass warrior who was part of an army of incredible women meant to face off against evil at the end of the world.

My front door swung open and shut. "Welcome to Chapel Comics," I called without looking up. "We close in five." I kept my tone friendly. Nothing was black and white, and it was possible to be polite without being walked on.

"We'll see." The words drew my attention, and my gaze lingered when I saw the man who stepped up to the counter. He was taller than my nearly six feet—a rare thing—and as broad in the shoulders as my father's most annoyingly sexy enforcer, Thac. A scar ran across his right eye, and the eye itself was clouded. In fact, scars covered him.

Looking him in the eye made my blood run cold, like thousands of years of ancient knowledge stared back, even though he was about the same age as my thirty.

Wasn't he?

He was sexy-scary in the same way as Thac, too.

But that didn't mean I was rewriting my rules because he came in late. "Fair point," I said. "We close now. Have a great night."

He didn't respond. Or really move at all.

A shiver ran down my spine. Did someone just walk over my grave?

I strode to the door and held it open for him. "Someone will be here at ten tomorrow morning if you'd like to come back. Probably. We'll see how tomorrow goes. Have a good night."

An unpleasant feeling tickled my thoughts, like spiders crawling over my brain. Ick. The way he was watching me, it was like that bad eye saw me more clearly than his good one.

"I'm sorry." His words sounded fuzzy. Why? "We got off on the wrong foot. I'll only be a few minutes. My niece loves Jean Grey, and I'm trying to find her the perfect present. The internet tells me you have the most unique collection this side of the country."

Every alarm in my head was screaming *warning,* and my mind drifted back to the encounter just a few weeks ago with the asshole stalking one of my students. Those memories were too fresh. Too vivid. I wanted to stand up to this guy, but I hadn't been able to handle it myself last time.

I'd sworn Thac was hanging around a lot lately. Not that I'd seen him, but it was like I could feel his presence. As if my dad had him checking on me more than normal.

Why the fuck wasn't he here now? He could jump out of the shadows any moment please and thank you.

"We have a fantastic selection," I said. "And someone would be happy to help you in the morning." *Please go. Please don't start something. Please don't be a crazy nut job who wants to trash the store. Why the fuck am I not tough enough to handle this myself?*

Caleb walked through the front door, which I still held. His dirty blond hair flopped over one eye when he gave me a bow. "Thank you, m'lady."

Thank you, *for coming home now.*

"I'll let you lock up, and come back tomorrow," the customer said, and brushed past Caleb on his way out.

Caleb turned to watch him leave, giving me a great view to distract me from the stress. His jacket hid the strength of his upper body, but when he turned to face me, I caught hints of muscle under his T-shirt, and his tattoo peeking from under the collar. "Did I interrupt something important?"

"Yes. Thank Jack Kirby, yes." One of my true gods. I clacked the deadbolt shut on the front door, and pulled the metal grate into place. I hated that I didn't handle that myself, but with Caleb it almost seemed all right.

He and I split up to yank the rest of the security fences down. It had taken me about a month of having my shop here to realize how strong people's feelings were about churches, especially those that weren't being used for worship.

Some people respected the structure, regardless. Others hated it regardless. And yet a different group of people wanted it to burn because I'd filled it with *filth*.

Please. Filth was what I daydreamed about Thac doing to me with a pair of handcuffs and his belt. The X-men were a poorly veiled metaphor for racism.

But haters were gonna hate, and that was why some of my stained glass was the original, peaceful scenes of sheep and flowers and sunlight, and other panes were inspired by the covers of my favorite comic issues.

"I take it Mr. Tall-Dark-and-Haunting wasn't a friend of yours?" Caleb asked when we finished, and met in the middle of the store.

I shook my head. "Just some creeper." With Caleb here, I felt comfortable closing out my drawer and counting out my deposits.

At first glance, he looked harmless, and that wasn't just because of the casual clothes and the black-rimmed glasses he watched me through. He was a couple of inches shorter than me, with a wiry build. His docile, pacifist attitude was deceptive, though. Not that he wasn't a pacifist, but there was something about him, an air of *I've seen more than I want you to know,* that I related to on a fundamental level.

We'd known each other for a few years. When he came in to talk to me about renting my spare room, I'd watched him disarm the gunman holding up my store, without so much as breaking a sweat. I was both in his debt for the save, and embarrassed I hadn't been able to take care of myself.

So similar to the situation with Mr. Bully a few weeks ago.

And everything about that was why I didn't charge him nearly as much rent as he should be paying.

"Oh, I brought dinner." Caleb picked up a plastic

bag from where he'd set it while he helped me. Steam collected on the inside. The print simply said *Thank You* again and again, but the delicious scent and shape of the containers inside told me it was Chinese. *Yummy.*

He plucked a DVD case from the bag, and shook it a couple of times to rid it of some of the condensation from dinner. "And Father Gregory asked me to liberate the donation box of this. Said it wasn't *family appropriate.*" Caleb worked for the still-active church down the street, teaching their immigrant members English as a second language.

The box said *Gremlins* on it, and an adorable-but-not-quite-right, fluffy little creature smiled back at us. This was the other reason I liked having Caleb here—he had the same taste in questionable movies that I did. "You're the best. Let me finish, and we'll screen that movie, to make sure it was right to take it out of unsuspecting hands."

Caleb shook his head, but he was smiling. "I'll go set us up, out back?"

"Be there in five."

Every few seconds I looked around. Someone was watching me; they had to be. Normally being alone in the comic shop didn't bother me, but the stranger had gotten under my skin. I still felt his presence as I wrote up deposit slips and locked everything in the safe for the night.

When I completed my tasks, I lingered at the back

door, one hand on the light switch and the other on the locked doorknob.

If I could be Jean Grey for just ten seconds, or Scarlett with her gorgeous new wings and Valkyrie powers, I'd take it. Right now. Long enough to keep me safe on the short walk from the church-turned-shop to the house out back.

Stop being a ridiculous child. I let the self-scolding echo in my head, shut off the power and locked everything up, and used the last of my willpower to walk at a brisk pace between the two buildings, rather than running like a madwoman.

I reached my door, and grasped the handle. Unlocked. Because Caleb was inside, and I was safe. My living room was decorated with an assortment of garage sale and curbside finds. The couch was threadbare under the quilt I kept draped over it, but it was comfortable. The paint flecked off the metal and glass stand the TV sat on, but it was sturdy.

There were two bedrooms down the hall—one for me, one for Caleb. The appliances in the kitchen were the newest things in the house, because my father had gifted me one thing after another, for birthdays and Christmas, when I refused to let him furnish the place.

The entire former preacher's house was smaller than the penthouse I'd been raised in, and it was the perfect home as far as I was concerned.

Caleb already had the takeout boxes spread

across the coffee table, using the bags as a makeshift tablecloth. He gestured to the food. "Your evening of decadence and bliss awaits, m'lady."

"Bliss? Gremlins?" I wasn't sure I agreed, but I left my keys in their spot by the door, and settled next to him on the couch. His thigh pressed into mine, and the heat was safe and tempting, but I'd learned a long time ago to not see more than friendship when nothing more was there.

"The company is the bliss. The gremlins are an excuse." He handed me a Styrofoam cup with broth and wontons inside, and a pair of chopsticks.

I wasn't going to correct him, even if it was over the top. "Where does the decadence come in?"

He leaned in with his mouth so near, his hot breath teased my cheek. "They gave us extra soy sauce," he whispered.

"Oh my God, the peasants will rebel when they discover how we're living."

Caleb grinned. "Pretty sure we're the peasants."

"Oh. Then don't tell the lords and ladies we've been gifted with such a bounty?"

He chuckled and grabbed the remote. "I promise it's just between us. Are you ready?"

"For all the awesome movie cheese we're about to have with our dinner? Of course."

Caleb started the DVD, and we dug into the food. This was every movie night with him—great spread on the table, flirting that didn't mean a thing, and all the banter a person could want.

I wouldn't mind if, once in a while, the evening ended with a little cuddling. Maybe some light fondling or some intense, incredibly hot sex. But I'd also learned long before I met Caleb that I wasn't the kind of woman men fell for. I was a little too weird. And big. And sometimes abrasive.

Sure, sometimes a guy would fuck me. Mostly because I was there, and they needed to get off. I did it for the physical affection. I wasn't willing to lose a great renter for something so base and primal. I didn't like living alone, and he was a good alternative.

He was also a good friend, though sometimes I was scared to admit that.

I shook the thoughts away, and when they tried to linger, I drowned them with a few large gulps of broth. The movie deserved my attention far more than my self-destructive thoughts did.

The old man had just finished explaining the rules of the mogwai to the dad, and Caleb said, "I had a friend like that once."

Like what? I looked between him and the TV. "Fluffy but cute, and not so great at communicating beyond grunts and chirps?"

"Grew more of himself when he got wet." Caleb's reply caught me off-guard.

I let out a bark of a laugh. "I do some interesting things when you get me wet, but so far, that's not one of them." Oh fuck. That sounded bad. It sounded exactly like what I meant, but I shouldn't have said it.

"Like what?" Caleb asked.

Best to laugh it off as a joke, rather than look awkward by taking it back. Besides, this was fun, and this was Caleb. He was safe. "Like randomly and repeatedly screaming out the name of the person who got me wet."

"That's a neat trick." Caleb smirked. "I'd like to see it sometime."

The flirting was normal with him. Like with Thac, it didn't mean anything. Caleb was being friendly and funny. That didn't stop me from wishing it meant more. "You also can't feed me after midnight, or I turn into a grumpy green monster."

"And yet, in the sunshine you practically glow." The way Caleb studied me felt like its own source of warmth.

There was an underlying sincerity in his words that stole my breath. I wasn't falling into that delusion though. "I have some really good sunscreen."

"Lucky for me."

I wanted to ask what he meant, but didn't dare interpret the words as anything more than a random comment.

Fortunately a loud crash from the screen yanked both of us back to the movie, and we laughed at our own jumpiness. As the film went on, we wrapped up dinner. We spent as much time making jokes and commentary as we did watching.

"Mia." Caleb's voice was soft, as he shook my shoulder. "Movie's over."

I wasn't sitting up. My cheek rested against something hard and textured. Caleb's thigh. When I moved, the throw from the back of the couch weighed in on me.

I'd fallen asleep during the movie, and he'd covered me up.

I scrambled upright at the realization.

"Whoa." Caleb's voice was still calm and quiet. "I didn't mean to startle you. I thought you might want to sleep in your own bed."

Right. Sure. I definitely did. "I'm sorry. I didn't mean to—" I snapped my jaw shut before I could ramble into a train of apology, but that didn't stop the embarrassment from flooding me.

"I didn't mind at all." Caleb sounded sincere.

I didn't dare believe he was being anything but polite. I stood more abruptly than I intended, and the throw fell to the floor. "Thank you for the movie. And dinner." I needed to stop acting like I had no self-control.

"Anytime. Really."

My brain was fuzzy. Images of Valkyries danced in my mind, and I was pretty sure I'd been dreaming of Caleb on top of me. Inside of me.

I'd been having filthy dreams about the person I

was sleeping on. My face heated to scorching. "I've got this. Cleaning up is the least I can do."

"It's not a problem." Caleb grabbed the throw from the floor as he stood and returned it to its spot on the couch.

"I've got this. I need to stretch a little anyway, after sleeping like that." I made my tone forceful.

Caleb looked like he was going to argue some more, but nodded. "You know where to find me if you need me." He headed into his room.

And if I pushed myself to clean-up, and forget the flashes of dream where he was making me very wet, I wouldn't need him.

I shoved trash into a plastic bag, and the boxes that still had food went in the fridge. Maybe taking the trash out would give me enough of a chill to chase away the lingering clouds of want.

I stepped outside, and a blast of cold hit me.

A loud caw cut through the night, startling me, and I jerked my head toward the sound. Two massive birds—ravens—sat on the bottom branch of a nearby tree. I swore they were watching me.

"Evening, gentlemen." I tipped my head in their direction. Ridiculous, but it made me feel better and helped me climb out of my thoughts.

The fact that their gazes seemed to follow me as I dumped the takeout boxes in the trash, then pushed into the house had me abruptly remembering my fear from the earlier visitor.

Sweet dreams, sister.

The words echoed in my head.

I locked the door behind me, though I swore I could still feel the ravens watching me.

What the fuck?

TWO
THAC (TLALOC)

Longing could be more excruciating than any wound suffered in battle.

I knew, because I was in love with my best friend's daughter, like something out of those intensely detailed romance novels that her best friend wrote.

All the way down to the fact that I was a centuries-old immortal, and she was a thirty-year-old human.

Fortunately, centuries of existence taught me patience and that there were times when I had to deny myself. I could keep her safe, regardless.

Her father did business in St. Louis, so I shouldn't be in the little town outside Albany, New York that she lived in. I shouldn't be near the comic shop he bought her when she asked to be free of him when she was twenty-one.

She thought he was some sort of movie-style crime

lord. He was certainly doing illegal things, but not according to human laws. He was an elf—a fae who made the mistake of breaking his people's rules by falling for a human, and was expelled from the fae realm for the sin.

Now he used his wealth and notoriety to help other outcasts like him stay out of the reach of whichever magical power they'd pissed off or needed to escape from. It was a concept I hadn't understood, something I couldn't forgive him for, until a few years ago.

When I reintroduced myself into his life was when I met Mia. The centuries had taught me that once individuals reached a certain level of maturity, a difference in age wasn't as important as a meeting of minds, and hers was as sexy as her body.

I wouldn't run into her tonight, despite being only a few blocks from her comic shop. It was likely she was watching movies with her renter. He was the reason for my visit. Since he moved in, the air around the church she did business in had changed. The protection and prosperity spells I'd put in place were still there, but there was a shift in all of it.

Inside, as well as out.

Not just on Caleb, but on Mia herself.

I was concerned she was manifesting her father's power, much later in life than she should be, and since it all started about the time she met Caleb, it was him I wanted to gather information on.

I slid into a booth in the all-night diner opposite the private investigator I'd hired to dig up information on Caleb. He might claim he was a struggling linguist, but his soul was something I'd never seen before. I wanted to know everything about who he was and where he'd come from, and when I went through my normal contacts, I found nothing.

A waitress approached before I was settled. "Can I get you boys something besides water? Are you waiting on anyone else?" Her tone was pleasant and chipper.

Jasper, the witch doing the investigative work for me, looked like he was about to climb out of his skin. "No." He clipped off the word.

"Coffee for me. And a slice of whatever your favorite pie is." I smiled warmly at Agnes. At least, that was who her name tag said she was. "Sure you don't want anything?" I asked Jasper. "It's on me."

"I'm good. Really."

He probably needed to lay off the coffee anyway. This wasn't how he'd acted last time I saw him.

"Be right back, hon." Agnes vanished into the back as if she were magic too, despite her being as completely human as everyone else in this town.

I mentally muttered a brief incantation, and wrapped her in a burst of prosperity. When I was a young god, hundreds of years ago, the people prayed to me for things like rain when their crops were thirsty, and sunshine when it was time to sow. They offered blood sacrifices in my name. They went to war for the favor of my siblings and me.

Blood sacrifices were rare these days, and I was no longer a fan. Kindness was also rare, though. I preferred to draw my power from faith in goodness, and in return, I blessed good people with the same. I did this for Ronan—Mia's father. I did it for someone like Agnes who was just *good* at her core.

And I offered the opposite as well, to those who were cruelly deceptive. Manipulative. I executed misery on behalf of those who couldn't find their own vengeance.

"Can we get this over with?" Jasper looked over his shoulder. In fact, he was spending more time looking around us than at me.

Interesting. "Certainly. Are you afraid of something?"

Jasper was working to get his investigation business off the ground, and I'd promised him a burst of success in exchange for this information. It was a fair deal—gods dealt in trades and favors all the time. "You didn't tell me who you were," he said.

"I told you exactly who I am."

"No." Jasper shook his head. "You didn't tell me who you worked for."

Ah. He'd found out about Ronan. "I don't work *for* him, I work *with* him. He isn't involved in this. He knows nothing about this."

"You have me looking into his daughter," Jasper hiss-growled.

"No. I have you looking into the man who rents a room from her." The distinctions were important. The fae may have cast Ronan out, making him an elf, but he'd been raised with their commitment to semantics. It was always *letter of the law,* never *spirit of the law.* "What did you find?"

"This Caleb guy is no one. Literally. He's got a bit of tragedy in his past, but don't we all? An orphan who found a good foster family when he was a toddler. They loved him. They raised him in their faith. They gave him everything and he acted like spoiled rich boys do as a teenager."

That could be dangerous for Mia on its own. "And?" I prompted.

"Kept up the rebellion through college. There were rumors of a fight club, but I never saw proof. And then he veered toward a more neutral ground a few years ago. Not immersing himself completely in his parents' faith, but no longer causing trouble either." Jasper started to rise.

I grabbed his wrist and urged him into his seat again. "Who were—"

"Here you go, boys." Agnes was back with Jasper's water, my coffee, and a delicious looking slice of lemon meringue pie.

Lemons in Albany in February. Modern life was wonderful. I handed her a twenty. "Thank you. You can take care of the bill for us, and keep the change."

"Of course, hon. But let me know if you need anything else. Stay as long as you'd like." Agnes walked away.

If Jasper had his way, he'd already be gone. I was curious to know what he thought he had to fear from Ronan, but that information wasn't part of our agreement, and I wanted my information more.

"Who were his birth parents?" I asked.

Jasper shook his head. "Couldn't find any information on them. Zero paper trail. He might as well have been left in a basket on the orphanage steps."

I was certain things didn't work that way in this modern world. The man had been born in an era of modern technology, and that meant there was a paper trail somewhere. "Find out."

"No. I'm done." Jasper stood again.

"You haven't brought me what you promised. Are you certain you want to make that decision?" I fixed him with a hard stare. There was no threat in my tone, but I knew what I looked like. Muscled. Scarred. Imposing.

Jasper jammed his hands into the pockets of his faux leather trench coat. "Can we work out a new arrangement? Something that calls us even? I don't want anything in return."

"What are you terrified of?" I had to know.

Jasper shook his head. "Please."

Intriguing. Even if I pushed him, it was unlikely anything else he brought me would be useful. "All right. We'll call this even, unless I find out you kept something from me that hurts her."

"I swear, I wouldn't. I'm not. I promise. Thank you." Jasper didn't stick around long enough for me to ask anything else.

He was far from the only being I'd encountered who was afraid of those I did business with.

I finished the pie and coffee, and was on my way. This would be a good time to leave town, but I didn't have any previous engagements and I wanted to see Mia.

That wasn't happening tonight, and neither was me sleeping.

With Jasper gone, I needed to find someone else to help me dig up information on Caleb. I'd exhausted my contact and favor lists, to locate Jasper, but there had to be someone I hadn't thought of.

There was a doorway in an alley a short distance from Mia's that looked like it led into an abandoned butcher shop. It actually led into the fae realm—specifically a pocket of the alternate plane of existence. With the right key, one could step into a door, find themselves here, and step out of the same door through one anywhere else in the world that had the same magics.

I planned to go back to Mia's in a few hours, but for now, I was going to enjoy this pocket of beauty, and meditate on my next steps. I placed myself a few feet from the doorway, tucked away from casual view, got comfortable on the lush green clover, and let my mind wander.

Hours later, I had no solutions, and it was time to go.

Mia always opened the door a few minutes early.

I walked into her shop right at ten, coffee in hand.

She had her back to me and jumped at the sound of the door, then laughed nervously when she saw me and tucked her long, dark hair behind one ear. A bright smile shone in her dark eyes. "Oh. It's you."

"Will you be happier to see me if I tell you I brought you a Valencia latte?" I held up the cup. I didn't know anyone else who drank it with just the orange, not the mocha, but she loved it.

She took the drink from me and repaid me with a kiss on the cheek. "I'm happy to see you regardless, but this makes you my bestest friend in the whole world in addition to being my savior."

"Hey now, bitch." Scarlett's voice came from the tablet near the register.

Apparently Mia had been FaceTiming with her actual BFF. "Besides you, skank." Mia blew a kiss at the screen.

"Now that your in-person protector is there, do you still want me to… You know? Send Pan and—?"

"I'm good now," Mia said. "I'll let you get back to work."

They told each other *goodbye,* and Mia turned to me.

"Why would she send you pans?" I asked. "And more importantly, why do you need a protector? What happened?" Was I wrong to take the night off?

"I'm fine now." She sipped her drink and leaned against the case behind her. The casual pose enhanced every curve I dreamed about riding on a regular basis.

I didn't appreciate the vague answer. "Were you not fine before? Tell me or I'll spank you until you give me the truth."

It had become clear to me a few years ago that she wanted me as badly as I did her. The number of times she called me when she was in trouble, the passes she made at me when she was drunk, or the simple *joking* requests to be tied up and used were all good indicators.

"You do that, and we'll be here for a long time." Mia bent enough to stick her gorgeous ass in my direction. "Best get started." She also thought muscular, tattooed guys like me didn't fuck tall, nerdy girls like her, despite how many times I'd told her that wasn't true.

It was a shame I couldn't show her how much I meant it. I tapped her lightly, though I wanted to do so much more. "How about you just tell me what was wrong?"

"Not a big deal. Some guy came in last night and

gave me a creepy vibe. Caleb scared him off, but I was worried he might come back this morning. Why are you in town?"

The change in subject didn't make me happy, and neither did the realization I hadn't prepared an excuse for being here. Careless of me. "Business, for your father. How much detail do you want?" The question was guaranteed to change the subject so I wouldn't have to lie to her too much—something I hated doing.

Her expression went blank. "None. In fact, that was too much."

Saved by her desire to be completely removed from a business that only existed in her mind.

I *really* hated keeping things from her. I also didn't want to end the conversation on that note. Mia was the reason I'd stopped by, and I was going to enjoy her company for at least a little longer. "However, even though business brought me to town, I'm *here* to see you."

"To check up on me?"

"Not in the way you mean."

She sipped her coffee and studied me over the lid. "How do I mean?"

"I'm not here to report back to Ronan. I wanted to see you. Make sure you're all right, for my own sanity."

Though I couldn't see her mouth, her smile reached her eyes. "I'm fine, see?" She held out her arms, coffee and all, and twirled. "Why wouldn't I be all right?" Suspicion was back in her voice.

I still wasn't certain, but I'd figure out the threat before it got to her. "It's my job to consider all possibilities."

"You mean it's your job to be paranoid," she teased. "I thought you weren't here for work."

"I'm not. That doesn't mean I stop thinking that way when I'm off the clock." I wrapped an arm around her waist and pulled her close, stealing her balance enough to make her squeal. I never lost my grip on her. This kind of playfulness skirted a line I should stay away from, but I couldn't behave all the time. "If that's what it takes to keep you safe…"

Mia lingered in my arms longer than she needed to, and her sigh was almost imperceptible when she pulled away. "Since you're here, do you have a few minutes to help me grab a few boxes from the back?"

"Of course." I followed her into the room where she stored backstock, and hefted the package she pointed out. "What does your calendar look like in two weeks?"

Mia scoffed. "I know which books are coming out, but you know I don't plan life out that far."

I not only knew it, but I'd also counted on it. "I have tickets to a midnight showing of *Rocky Horror Picture Show*."

"No. Really? No." She led me back into the main shop.

"Really truly." I'd picked them because we loved watching the movie together, and she'd always wanted to live the full experience.

"That means you'll be back." Mia gestured for me to set the box down, and she opened it.

I handed her items one at a time for her to put away. "I wouldn't miss this for anything."

She hummed "Time Warp" as she put collectibles in their spots. Seeing her like this, content and in her element, was one of the best sights I could witness.

While we were working, Caleb returned. The look he gave me was one of caution, but his greeting to Mia was friendly.

I didn't like having him here—ever but especially now. He was a threat, even if I had yet to prove it, but there was a compelling air about him. And he was attractive. Not in the all-consuming way Mia had my attention, but pretty to look at.

"You're in a good mood," Caleb said to her.

She twirled, still humming the song, and grabbed his hand. "Thac is taking me to see Rocky Horror."

He gave me another appraising look, his gaze lingering longer this time.

I stared back, challenging with my gaze.

Caleb turned back to Mia. "You're a lucky girl."

She pulled him into the dance for a few steps before letting him go.

A spike of possessiveness pierced me at the sight, and I had to clench my jaw to bite back the *hands off,* that tried to force its way out. I wouldn't rip his hand from hers. Mostly because she'd already let go, but the insistence was still necessary in my head.

My phone buzzed in my pocket, and I fished out the device.

Where are you? Ronan asked.

I typed a quick reply. *Be there in ten.*

"I have to run," I said to Mia. "Work beckons. I'll send you details about the show." I kissed her on the cheek. As I walked from her shop, I forced myself to leave the thoughts of *mine* behind me. She wasn't. She couldn't be.

It might take more than a few solid thoughts to convince myself of that, though.

THREE
CALEB

HEAT.

So much intensity.

I tried to push the traces of my dream aside, but I still felt it everywhere. The splash of blood on my arms. The clawing need throbbing in my cock. The pain. The desire.

The details of what I'd envisioned in my sleep were gone, but the feelings lingered on my skin. I forced my eyes open and ignored the ache of my insistent erection as I sat up in bed. It had been a long time since I had a dream like that, and I didn't care for it at all.

Usually the simple decor of my room—plain pale walls, plain pale sheets, soft gray carpet and as few possessions as possible on the bookshelves—was enough to ground me and quiet any stray thoughts. Tonight, it was more of an assault on my senses. The copper tang of a good fight lingered in my nostrils and a roar echoed in my ears. A battle. A vicious one.

I could taste salt and sweat and blood. Could see it splashed in ghosted images across my room. And the rush that tingled on my skin had my gut churning with nausea and the reminder of how much pain I'd caused people when I was younger.

A glance at my phone told me it was three in the morning. I wasn't going back to bed anytime soon. Instead, I forced one foot in front of the other and into the bathroom.

Stripping out of what little clothing I slept in brought back another surge of disgust, on a wave of my subconscious thought. My half hard dick gave a weak salute. The temptation to walk across the hall, to see if Mia wanted to help me address the erection, surged forward on a wave of want.

Moments like this, when my willpower was weak and my mind was exhausted, it was a struggle to ignore my attraction to her. She wasn't interested, and she'd laughed off my advances more than once, so these days I limited the suggestions to teasing.

And pretended I could sate the desire for her by jerking off to fantasies of her tight, slick pussy wrapped around my dick, after she and I retired to our own rooms at night.

I ignored my bastard of a cock as I stepped into icy cold water. The chill jarred me the rest of the way to consciousness and left my teeth chattering, but it didn't rinse away the dense cloud in my mind.

I dried off because it was necessary to keep me from getting sick when I went out in the cold, and not because I had any motivation to add another layer of sensation to my already overloaded body. Coming down with a cold would mean fever dreams and that was the last thing I wanted.

I dressed in heavy jeans and a sweatshirt, and grabbed my coat. A walk would help me clear my thoughts and if it didn't, the weather might numb them.

Mia's bedroom door was closed as I crept into the hall. Even if the thought of waking her up didn't fill me with immense desire, this wasn't something I could talk to her about. We shared a lot—I knew who her father was, and she knew how much I'd struggled with my sexuality in the past, thanks to a religious upbringing and the serious trauma of losing my first not-boyfriend to suicide.

But she wouldn't understand the lingering guilt. That when my defenses were down and I was exhausted, I would hover on that line between being disgusted by the man I'd been, the man who was willing to hurt anyone and anything to feel, and wanting to embrace him again. She'd had her beliefs questioned again and again, and somehow still believed there was enough good in the world to save it.

I hoped she was right.

An icy blast hit my face as I stepped outside. Something to focus on that wasn't inside my head. *Thank you, God.* No place was open this early except the convenience store at the corner of the street Mia's shop sat on, and a diner five blocks over.

Neither one of those would offer solace.

I tried to focus on anything outside my mind. The crunch of ice under my boots, as I trudged down the road. The way the streetlights reflected off patchy snow in large circles. Sometimes I'd step into a patch of darkness, or a flickering ring of light—a metaphor for my life?

We lived at the edge of the city, and my aimless wandering took me past an assortment of old brick buildings mixed with new glass and concrete.

I stopped at the sight of concrete steps to my right. The church.

My adopted parents had raised me to love their god. As a teenager, I realized I was attracted to men as much as I was to women, and the conflict their faith caused with my desire had wreaked havoc on my thoughts. I lashed out in a search for answers, and all these years later I still regretted the things I'd done swinging from one extreme to another.

I turned to face the building, letting my gaze follow the spires up to the sky. Even in the darkness, the stained glass above the entrance sparkled with a haunting beauty. The intricately carved doorway seemed to beckon to me.

As a child I thought peace was inside that building. As a young adult, I only saw it as torment. These days, it was simply quiet, and sometimes my brain needed that.

I'd tried more than a decade ago to crawl my way back to faith, but I'd changed too much. Seen too much. And I'd spent the past several years trying to find the balance between violent, angry me, and the me who just wanted to live and let live.

A sharp chill raced up my spine, as a bird cawed from the shadows.

Inside would be far better than outside, so I strode quickly up the steps and through the front doors. I slipped into the chapel, letting the warmth penetrate my icy skin. The pews were empty, aside from one priest sitting up front and praying. The air in here was comfortable, or would be soon. Once my thoughts calmed. Once I found my center.

Once the faint images and drive for fire and ice stopped flashing in my mind.

I shed my coat and set it on the pew next to me in the middle of the chapel, then took a seat. Hands clasped, and forearms resting on the back of the bench in front of me, I bowed my head.

I didn't have the same kind of faith my parents did. Life had shown me too much, for me to blindly follow their religion. But there were still pieces I believed were right and real. Concepts like kindness and acceptance that were worth hanging onto.

Please. Fill me with your peace. Calm my fractured soul. I'm your humble servant. All you ask is yours. Please grant me this in return.

I didn't know who I was praying to—their god or another. The words made me feel like someone was listening, though.

"Oh." A soft voice disrupted my prayer.

I looked up to see a woman about my age standing a few rows behind me.

She must have moved like the wind for me to not have heard the door open and close when she came in. I tried to focus on her, and for a moment a blurred image overlapped her face. I rubbed my eyes to rid them of the dragon from my dream, and this time she was just her.

"Sorry." She ducked her head. "I didn't mean to intrude. I was just surprised to see anyone else here." Her pale skin had red splotches, presumably from the cold. Platinum blond hair peeked out from under the hoodie pulled over her head.

And there was a sadness to her. I wasn't sure how I knew, but I'd always had an instinct for things like that—sadness, despair, confusion. Feelings I understood more intensely than I wanted to.

Perhaps listening to someone else would help ease my burdens. "There's room for both of us." I gestured at the vast, empty space with only two people in it. "Or I'm here to listen if you need an ear."

"I won't disturb your time with Him." She slipped into a pew across the aisle, and sat, her coat pulled tight around her and her gaze on the crucifix that hung at the head of the room, behind the altar.

I returned to my meditations. As I recited memorized prayers in my head and grounded myself in the room around me, the oppressive dream slowly bled away, and calm slipped into my thoughts to take its place.

"Peace is not where you're seeking it." The words were whispered in my ear, carried on a soft, unfamiliar voice.

My eyes flew open, and I scanned the room. The woman was gone, and the sky outside the windows was pale gray, instead of black and suffocating.

How long had I been here?

I grabbed my coat and stood to tug it on. When the rustling of my movements quieted, a soft sound reached my ears. Crying?

I turned and was surprised to see the blonde was still here, but she'd moved to a back pew. Her sadness and feeling lost were tangible, not just because of her tears.

I moved closer, and sat next to her. She didn't look up.

"I'm happy to listen," I said. "In here, anything that's said is between us. It never leaves these walls."

Once upon a time I was going to be a priest. I'd even gone to seminary for a few years. I was going to make my parents proud, finally.

Though I'd fallen away from the religion, I still believed people should have a friendly ear when they needed one. But I also believed whoever was listening should *only* listen and not judge.

She let out a slow sigh. "This isn't the kind of thing I can talk about."

"Okay." Pushing wouldn't do me much good. Being here would.

"Not because I don't want to, but… It's hard to explain."

I nodded, though she wasn't looking at me. "I understand."

"You really don't." Her laugh was bitter and tainted.

I did. There were a lot of things I couldn't talk about. Things most people should understand, but so very few of them wanted to see.

"Do you ever feel like your entire life has been a lie?" she asked.

Most definitely. When I started to recognize my bisexuality, I wondered why I'd been cursed, and when I swung away from the guilt, I wondered why so many people insisted loving someone with the *wrong* genitalia wasn't right. "Yes. For me, in some cases it was a matter of needing to shift my perspective, and in other cases, there were falsehoods I needed to accept."

She finally looked up at me with eyes so bright, so clear, they looked like chrome in this lighting. She tilted her head, and they went back to blue. "I think this is a case of both, but I'm not sure… What if I can't accept it? How do you look reality in the eye and say, *I see you, but you're a lie*?"

That wasn't the kind of question that had an easy answer. If I were talking to a friend, someone who understood my sense of humor, I'd quote Seth Gecko in *From Dusk Till Dawn. I don't believe in vampires, but I believe in my own two eyes, and what I saw is fucking vampires.*

I doubted this woman would appreciate the reference, or that it was relevant. "You don't. Not if you know it's real."

"But what about faith?" she asked.

Faith lies. People lie. Life is a series of chances to adjust our perspectives and learn and grow, and if there is a higher power out there, don't you think that's what they want for us? "Each person's faith is personal. The right answer for me may not be the right one for you."

"What if someone proved to you that dragons were real?" she asked.

I swallowed my chuckle. As a child, I would've followed that person anywhere. "Dragons are as real as Santa." As I spoke, a forgotten snippet of my dream clanged in my head. A phantom ache echoed in my fingers.

She gave me a smile that didn't reach her eyes and stood. "Thank you for listening." She walked from the church.

Chase her down. Learn more. Make her prove it.

The insistent voice in my head wasn't mine. It was the same roar I gave into when I was younger. The temptation that used to tell me the endless nights of fighting were all right. The pain—mine or someone else's—was worth it.

That worked for some people, but it had nearly destroyed me. Especially the violence. The world didn't like a violent man, even if the people I acted out against asked for it or deserved it.

I certainly deserved it.

An ache in my palms, a dampness, jarred me from the thoughts before they could spiral. I flexed my fingers and looked at my hands. Were those claws retracting? Actual cuts in my skin?

No. Another look didn't show either one to be true, but blood welled up in my palms from wounds that didn't exist.

The dream slammed into me again, knocking my thoughts off-kilter, and I forced it aside.

Time to go home, drink a lot of coffee, and make sure I stayed alert and conscious for the next several hours. Long enough to shake off this disconcerting feeling.

FOUR
MIA

I SWORE I HEARD CALEB GET UP AT A HORRIFIC HOUR this morning, but I hadn't been able to shake off the sleep enough to check on him. He was gone when I finally got out of bed around six. Wherever he'd gone, I hoped he was all right.

Some mornings it felt like everything was moving in slow motion. Even though I had an employee opening the store this morning, and my schedule was my own, everything was taking just a little too long.

The whole tone of the morning was *I'm running late* despite only being beholden to me and my own time.

My shitty dreams weren't helping my fractured brain any. Half the night my subconscious taunted me with images of Scarlett's new Valkyrie life. Kirby, who supposedly gave Scarlett her powers, was there. I'd never met the woman, but my mind had given her a face, apparently.

The creepy one-eyed guy from the shop two nights ago was there too, along with a pair of ravens.

And the entire scene was a massive battle straight out of a comic book. Vast and ridiculous, like in a Marvel movie, but I was stuck in the middle of it. I was lost and confused and didn't know what to do. I didn't want to fight. I wanted to heal. Help.

Save.

It was the kind of dream I should be able to shake off, but the helpless feeling lingered while I got ready for the day, and even after I stepped out into the cold, to head to the coffee shop down the street. As I walked, I flipped through a short stack of hardback graphic novels I'd gotten in yesterday afternoon.

I pushed through the front door of the coffee place with my shoulder, the way I had dozens of times before.

A sharp, "Watch it," yanked my attention from the books, and I fumbled to keep them from falling from my arms.

"Sorr—" The apology died on my lips when I found myself face to face with someone I'd never met, but I felt like I knew as well as anyone. According to my subconscious, this was Kirby. "I dreamt about you."

Idiot. Why was I such a dunce sometimes?

Someone hit my shoulder hard, catching me off-guard and knocking the books from my arms. "Damn it."

The random man kept walking toward the counter, not sparing me so much as a glance.

"I've got it." The man with maybe-Kirby crouched and had most of the books gathered before I could move. He finished, stood again, and handed me the stack. He was barely taller than me. Probably about as wide, but his bulk looked like solid muscle. The blond hair, tattoos peeking up above the collar of his shirt, and faded scars made him look like a modern-day Viking.

When he handed me my books, his jacket sleeve pulled up above his gloved hand, exposing his wrist, and I swore I caught a glimpse of twisted, metallic looking flesh. If he had a prosthetic, he didn't move like it.

"We were looking for you." Maybe-Kirby's voice drew my attention.

Me? Why in God's name…?

Fuck. "Did something happen to Scarlett? Is she hurt? I was just talking to her yesterday." Did Pan know? Did Arnlaug? "Wait?" I didn't even know this was Kirby. And if it was, "Why did you come to me to tell me that?" Yeah, Scarlett was my best friend, but an in-person visit, when Scarlett had other people in her life who she was closer to—who she *lived* closer to…

"Scarlett's fine last time I checked." Maybe-Kirby almost sounded amused. "I'm here to talk to *you*."

That didn't sound right. The maybe-queen-of-the-Valkyries and her scary man wanted to talk to *me*. Did Valkyries have queens? If they did, she was waiting for my answer.

"I was about to get some coffee, if you want to join me. Unless you're leaving," I said.

"We're staying." The man spoke with the authority of someone used to being listened to.

The woman offered her hand. "I'm Kirby, by the way."

"Mia." This was such a strange encounter. Then again, even magical creatures deserved politeness—That was something my father told me many times as a child.

If he had any idea…

"Starkad." The man offered his hand too.

I wanted to ask about the hint of not-really-flesh I saw peeking out, but that wouldn't be polite, so I shook his hand as well.

Crap, we were still blocking the doorway. I moved further into the shop. "Can I get either of you coffee? Anything else?" Always be polite. That was my father's overall message. Always be a good hostess. They were here to see me, even if we weren't in my *home*.

"I'll get the coffee. The two of you sit," Starkad said. "What are you drinking?"

His attitude grated across me, which was odd. He wasn't being rude, but his posture and tone reminded me of the people who worked for my father. The man who had made my childhood miserable. The bully who had come into my shop a few weeks ago looking for a student. None of that was Starkad's fault. It did put me on edge though.

Besides, another of my father's lessons was to never accept a gift until I knew the terms. Especially when it came to food. "I've got my own, thanks."

I wasn't trying to be a bitch—those were simply The Rules.

Kirby found us a seat, while Starkad and I waited to get drinks. It was weird standing silently next to him, but I had no idea what kind of conversation to make.

Do you turn into a bear too? A wolf? How long have you been an enforcer? Are you billions of years old, or are you a new immortal like Scarlett? What happened to your hand? Which one of you is the top?

All of those felt like the equivalent of asking a stranger how much they made or weighed. Sure, some people would do it, but that didn't make it the right way to talk to people you just met.

So, like a lump, I stood in line and fluctuated between trying to look like I wasn't ignoring him, and not saying anything.

I ordered the breakfast sandwich and a muffin to

go with my orange coffee, while he got one black coffee and one caramel mocha.

They might be able to live off bean juice alone, but some of us had chunky figures to maintain.

Orders in hand, we joined Kirby. Starkad took the spot next to her, and I sat across from them.

"What can I do for you?" I asked.

The instant one of them sipped their coffee, that meant I was okay to eat. I dug into my sandwich.

"I understand Scarlett told you..." Kirby twisted her mouth. "About who she is?"

Was she disappointed in Scarlett? No. It was my understanding this wasn't a massive *never tell anyone* secret, even though it wasn't the kind of thing the general population was ready to hear.

So Kirby was feeling out how much I knew before she told me more. If, for some weird reason, this was a totally different Kirby who just happened to look the same as the person I dreamed turned Scarlett into a Valkyrie, and who also knew her name, then what I was going to say next would either sound like a joke or be expected regardless.

"About her wings?" I asked. "About her being a Valkyrie? About magical beings, walking among us like real -life comic -book characters?"

Kirby sipped her drink, but the action didn't completely hide her smile. "Yes. That."

The way Starkad sat there, silent, watching, almost statue-like, put me on edge. He radiated *I know I'm intimidating*, like the men who worked for my father. Men who used fear and unspoken threats, to get things done. Men who picked on insecure teenage girls and laughed about it.

I didn't like it. "What's his deal?" I nodded at him. That same kind of person rarely liked having attention drawn to them. "Is he here to look badass? Or to tell me if I don't keep my mouth shut, *things* will happen?"

Starkad's brows knit together. It was scary—I'd give him that.

I'd seen worse.

"No," Kirby said. "He looks like that by default. He spent the last decade having to pretend he was a tattooed asshole who was manically in love with me, and he's happy to be himself again."

Not the answer I expected.

Starkad rolled his eyes. "I *am* a tattooed asshole who's madly in love with you."

"Not *like that,* though." Kirby nudged him playfully.

Okay, that was kind of cute. The type of simple gesture that said, *we're comfortable with each other, regardless of what the rest of the world thinks.*

Which was enviable.

"Did you come to find out how much Scarlett told me?" I finished off my sandwich and stared at my muffin. Should I show a little restraint and save it for later? "I promise I haven't told anyone else—not that anyone would believe me."

Kirby shook her head. "That's not why we're here either. Rather, we will discuss that, but mostly so I know how much more information you need. It's a result, not my mission."

Mission. A weird word to use. I didn't like the gnawing in my gut; it wasn't one that said, *Eat the muffin.* It was more like, *Your world is about to be shattered.*

"I want to make you the same offer I made Scarlett. I want you to be a Valkyrie," Kirby said.

I let out a barking laugh so loud I drew stares from the other tables.

Oops.

The people looking at us seemed to decide after a few seconds that we weren't worth the attention and went back to their drinks and conversations.

"That's not funny, but it's also hilarious." I couldn't help another snort. "Did Pan put you up to this?"

"She's one-hundred-percent serious." Starkad didn't look like he did jokes.

But that would be part of the prank, wouldn't it? "Okay. Whatever. Why are you here?" I asked Starkad. "You weren't with Kirby when she approached Scarlett."

"She has her own berserker." Starkad said the line with a straight face.

Kirby didn't seem in a hurry to finish the sip of coffee she was taking. She finally set the cup down. "That's really good. Not as good as the place in North Carolina… I'll take you sometime, Mia. But to answer your question, he's here to make you feel more comfortable."

"Does he make anyone feel more comfortable? Besides you?" I was missing something.

"No," Starkad said. "But you're not other people."

Wait. So he was here for the same reason I didn't want him here? "Because of my father?" I wasn't sure how I knew that, but the answer seemed clear. "How much do you know about me?"

There were things I'd never told Scarlett, and that was one of them. *Hey, my dad's in organized crime* was a different level of secret than, *I'm a Valkyrie now.* One just meant a little bit of a mental evaluation, if the wrong person thought we believed it, and the other got people put in prison.

Namely, my dad.

"We only know what a little in -depth on-line digging turned up." Kirby ignored her drink and focused on me.

The milk steamer hissed, and silverware clattered against porcelain, and people around us chatted, and not a single one of those people had any idea how insane our conversation was.

"This isn't funny, whatever it is. Why would you want this"—I gestured at myself—"to be a Valkyrie?"

I definitely wanted the muffin. I pulled the wrapper off and stuffed a large portion of the bottom of the sweet in my mouth.

"I want you because of what's in your heart." Kirby sounded sincere. She also sounded straight out of an after-school special.

I wasn't buying it. "Sorry to be the one to tell you, but even if my heart was willing, my flesh is weak. I'm not Valkyrie material."

"Are you certain?" Starkad asked.

Was I…? Was *he* serious? "Are you going to shame me into accepting? Because that seems contrary to your ultimate goal."

"Here's the basic intro," Kirby said. "There's a war coming—Ragnarök is real."

"Yeah, and funny as hell. Though I was more of a *Guardians* fan." Bringing comic books to life was one of the best things ever, if only they would stop fucking up Jean Grey.

Kirby snorted a laugh. "Don't let Magnus hear you say that."

"Who the fuck is Magnus?" Oh wait. The guy from those books they kept making bad adaptations of. No, that couldn't be right.

"She's one of us," Kirby said. "A Valkyrie. Look, bad things are about to unfold that most of the world doesn't know about, and we'd like to keep people—the unknowing, the unwitting, the normal people, and the magical people who don't want to be involved—from dying."

"Basically, you're raising an army of magical girls." None of this sounded appealing.

Why did I want to accept, then?

Because her delusion was rubbing off on me. "I'm too old and too big and too awkward to look good in a skintight fuku, wings or not. I promise you want someone else on your team," I said.

"She came to you because she wants you." Starkad didn't look as amused as Kirby. Or any level of amused. If he smiled, would his face crack?

I wasn't dealing with him. I kept my attention on Kirby. "I appreciate the offer, even if it's a joke."

"It's not. I'm sincere." All traces of laughter were gone from her expression.

Uh-huh. "What are the odds that you sought out my BFF first and then came for me just a few weeks later? How plausible is that?"

"What are the odds that you're best friends with a woman who lives halfway around the world, and you only know each other because she happened to have a book signing—her first—at your shop? Fate drives a lot of us together. Whatever is pulling the strings, whoever pushes to make these things happen… I'm honestly surprised more of you didn't know each other already."

Magic was real. Scarlett had proven that to me, but this…

I wanted what Kirby said to be the truth. I wanted it to be in my future and reality.

But I knew who and what I was, and the world didn't work the way she was describing.

"Thanks, but you need someone else." I picked up my things, including the partly eaten muffin, and walked out.

Kirby didn't try to stop me.

Was I making a mistake?

As I walked toward the comic shop, a raven flew across my path, and landed on the bench just a few feet away. The way he watched me, I swore there was an intelligence in his gaze.

I set the muffin in front of him, and was surprised when he gave it a few pecks instead of flying away.

"I hope you like carrot," I said and continued my walk back to my shop.

I swore I heard, *Next time bring chocolate -chip,* whispered on the wind.

Because now the ravens were talking to me?

That was almost as ludicrous as the idea of me being a Valkyrie.

FIVE
THAC

I NEEDED TO FIND SOMEONE NEW TO GET ME information on Caleb. It was a shame I didn't have an excuse to insert myself into Mia's life for more than a few hours at a time, as that would let me watch him and be closer to her. I also needed to figure out who told Jasper about me, and why my ties had him spooked.

I grabbed a mead from a rack in the kitchen—a local place made a blend with just a hint of berry—and settled in the recliner in the living room. At first glance the chair looked like it came off a showroom floor, but the leather was hunted and tanned by a craftsman who respected the land. The wood underneath was the same. Most of the furnishings in my apartment were like that.

Though I did have a few modern addictions. Television, for instance. I loved mixed martial arts, and hated *survival* shows when it was clear they weren't really working for it. And I enjoyed yelling at both.

Overall though, the elements of my home, the care that had gone into making them and the materials they contained, made me feel closer to what lay under the city. It reminded me that more than concrete and glass used to be here.

Whom else could I call about the Caleb mystery? What favors were owed me? Which bridges wouldn't be burned if my contacts found out I was working with Ronan again?

My cell phone rang, and I fished it from my pocket. Once upon a time, the only way to get my attention across long distances was to offer a prayer carried on potent faith. This was easier, but that didn't mean I had any appreciation for it.

The name *Carmen* showed on the screen, and I clicked *Answer*. "Hola."

"Tio. I'm sorry to bother you." Stress hung heavy in her tone and slunk through the line. She spoke with a distinct Spanish accent, but her English came easily.

I was both pleased and disappointed she'd adapted so quickly to life here. It had only been about ten years, but she might as well have been in Arizona since she was a child. I wasn't actually her uncle, though most everyone in her family called me that. A lot of gods, regardless of where they were from, chose to have families at various points as they walked more and more with humanity, but I wasn't one of them. "It's fine, always. What's wrong?"

"It's not fine. Abuelita says we're not to bother you, but I didn't know who else to call."

Years ago, when Carmen's grandmother, Fatima, was young, before she'd met the man she would marry—before she had any spark of what her future held——I'd dated her. Something I'd done off and on over the centuries, always looking for that deeper connection, but never finding it with a mortal. Fatima was the last human I tried that with, and in the end, our parting was amicable, and she'd gone on to live a vivid, mortal life.

"Tell me what's wrong." I deepened my tone. Pushed more force into the words.

Carmen sighed, and a string of muffled profanities greeted me. "I'm sorry. It's Lucia. She's been arrested. She's in Nevada, and I don't know anyone in the area. I don't know what to do. How to bail her out. I don't... *Damned* child."

"It's okay. I'll get her." There was no hesitation in my offer. Though the family wasn't mine by blood, they were still family. "Tell me where she is and what happened."

"I don't know what happened. She's supposed to be visiting Abuelita, but she called and said she needed to be bailed out. She refused to talk about why. She's got these *friends*..." Another string of muffled curses. "Thank you." Carmen gave me the jail information, we said our *goodbyes*, and hung up.

She didn't ask how I planned to get to the other side of the country quickly, and I didn't offer the information. They didn't know I was a god, but one of the unspoken rules with their family was that they didn't ask how I accomplished certain things, and I didn't offer answers.

I spent a few moments changing into a nicer suit. Making sure I looked like a wealthy, presentable American. It was never an issue for me to intimidate people, but things would go more smoothly for me and for Lucia if I dressed and acted a certain way when I went to pick her up.

The thought almost made me chuckle. I was a fucking god. Once upon a time, I would've stood in front of whoever was in charge, suggested that they could choose between prosperity or drought, and taken Lucia back to her family without argument.

The world had changed so much over the centuries.

I made my way down to the street, stepped into a door that should lead nowhere, and stepped out onto a small street in Ely. No one questioned that I'd just walked out of a door they'd never really noticed before. In a building that didn't have a business in it. No one else would try to walk through that same door.

It was part fae magic and part human nature. Very

few people saw what they didn't want to, and spells on the door amplified that. Their gaze would glance off the spot as if it never existed, unless they were looking very hard for the location I just came from.

I would have preferred the path drop me closer to my destination, but with travel like this, I took what I could find.

There was snow on the ground, but the day was bright, and the several-block stroll in the sunshine felt good on my face. A short while later, I walked into the jail and told the man at the front desk that I was here for Lucia Amo. I confirmed that yes, I was her uncle, and of course I had the ID to prove it. Ronan had made sure of that.

The man took my information and the money for bail, though he did it all with skepticism. A moment later, someone went to get Lucia, and I sat to wait.

Once upon a time, when there were hundreds of thousands of them at once, the prayers were a voiceless chorus. These days, with so few remembering the old ways and keeping the old faith, I recognized each and every person who muttered my name in praise or curse or in search for mercy.

Fatima had prayed to me her entire life. She didn't know her former lover and one of her gods were the same individual, and as time went on, she only ever offered praise for her prosperity. Thanks for her family and life.

Until about ten years ago, when her gratitude

became a plea for help. The small town where she and her family lived had become dangerous. She wanted a new life for them, before she passed and couldn't take care of them anymore. She was in her eighties at that point, and had a couple of great grandchildren, including Lucia.

I'd heard the request and it was one I couldn't deny. Not for such a pure, kind soul.

I couldn't move an entire group of people that large, and even if I could, I didn't have the type of power required to set them up in a new location, with a new life.

But Ronan did. He'd been asking me to come back and work with him. Insisting he'd severed the ties with the followers of Malsumis—the reason I'd stopped dealing with him to begin with. So I agreed to return, if he would help Fatima and her family find a new, safe life.

I brought them through a temporary gate, big enough and open long enough for them to move through two countries in a single step. They didn't know I was a god, but their family embraced old magics, and didn't question the trip. Ronan set them and me up with new identities, and in return, I worked with and for my old friend again.

"Tio." Lucia's cheerful greeting echoed across the tile.

I turned to see her half-walking, half-skipping

toward me, a grin on her face, and scooped her into a big hug. "Idiotic child." My words were affectionate.

"I know. I'm sorry."

I set her on her feet again. "Explain when we're outside." It wasn't a request.

She gave a brief nod, we finished signing her out and getting her things, and we were on our way.

"Where's your car?" I asked when we stepped outside.

"Back at my motel." She gestured in the same direction I'd just come from.

We started walking. "Good. Then you have time to explain what happened."

"It wasn't my fault. Some puta grin—"

I silenced her with a look. "Would you use that language in front of your mother?"

"Who do you think taught it to me?" Most of the time, Lucia was clearly an intelligent woman in her early twenties, and other times, she was still the sassy twelve -year -old I met for the first time when I helped the family come here.

Right now she was a petulant blend of both, with her graceful walk and indignant pout. "Fine." She huffed. "This perfectly-kind-under-other-circumstances-I'm-sure white lady bumped me with her car when I was crossing the street. I smacked the hood of her car as *thanks,* and may have muttered a choice word or two, that left a Hulk-fist sized dent. She told the cops I jumped on her car and threatened to beat her up."

Like her great-grandmother, Lucia was a bruja, and had just enough natural magic to be dangerous when she let her temper run hot.

In this case, I saw nothing wrong with her response. "Good girl." I ruffled her hair.

She grinned. "I'm really sorry you had to come all the way out here for me, though. Mom's going to try to repay you, but don't let her. Please? Let me make it up to you instead."

I nodded my acceptance. That seemed fair, and I may have just found a solution to another problem. I didn't want Lucia going anywhere near Caleb, but if she had any ideas… "There's a man I need more information about."

"Ooh, a secret, scary man?" Lucia's tone was exaggerated fright. "A terrifying, sexy man?"

"No." Not as far as I needed her to know. "But I think he's hiding something, and I'm wondering if you know of any ways to see things like that, without alerting him."

She grinned. "I have the perfect solution. You have to come with me to visit Bisabuela, though."

"You don't counter a favor by asking for another favor." I didn't have to teach her that. If she didn't understand the give and take of balance, she'd have a lot worse problems than my temper. I'd been putting off visiting Fatima, though.

As her dementia had gotten worse over the last few years, I'd made sure her family could put her in the highest end care facility. But in my mind, she was still the young woman who looked almost exactly like Lucia. Who was bright and sunshine and full of faith. I didn't like seeing her mind go.

"It's not a favor for me," Lucia said. "This is because she's been asking for you. It's a favor for her. Besides, she has a camera, and you need that to take pictures of this mysterious person of yours, and then I can look and tell you what I see."

"I have a camera in my phone." I may be ancient and a little behind the times, but I wasn't completely out of the technology loop.

Lucia rolled her eyes. "Good for you. Me too. But the camera I need is special."

Never argue with a witch about her tools. "All right," I agreed.

"Excellent." Lucia clapped. "I'm driving."

A given, since I didn't drive. I folded myself into the passenger seat of her old Honda, and we were on our way. The trip consisted of a lot of singing to the radio and chair dancing. Most of the latter was Lucia, since I wasn't going anywhere in my seat until the car stopped.

We reached the care facility and headed inside. Lucia had a smile and a wave for most everyone, and most of them seemed to recognize her. A few even stopped and asked if I was her new man. She made a disgusted face each time and explained I was her uncle.

That so few already knew that was a good indicator I hadn't visited enough. Fatima was not only the last mortal I'd been with, but also the other reason I wouldn't let anything happen with Mia. I could see myself falling for her, then watching her brief life pass in a blink, and losing her before I knew it.

Mia deserved someone who would grow old with her. Someone who would understand that part of being human.

Lucia knocked on Fatima's door, and pushed inside when there was no answer. "Bisabuela?" Lucia called softly.

Fatima sat in a large chair near the window, her gaze fixed on nothing in particular.

Lucia knelt next to her. "Bisabuela, look who I brought to see you."

Fatima blinked, but otherwise, there was no response.

I hated seeing her once-brilliant mind reduced to this.

Lucia didn't look fazed. She chatted, keeping up one side of what should be a two-sided conversation, while she straightened her great-grandmother's pillows. Made sure the older woman was comfortable. After about fifteen minutes, Fatima still hadn't responded.

Lucia gave her a kiss on the cheek. "Tio and I are

going now. I'm taking your camera. You call me if you need anything."

"Stay." Fatima focused on me, and like that, there was a lucidity in her gaze. "Thac, stay for a few minutes, please."

My breath caught, and I nodded. "Of course."

"I'll be in the car." Lucia squeezed my hand and walked from the room.

I knelt in front of Fatima and took one of her hands between mine. Her skin was thin. Papery and cold. When she was like this, however, I could see the girl I used to know in her eyes.

She rested her free hand on my cheek. *"My blessed Tlaloc,"* she said in Spanish. *"It's been so long."*

I was surprised to hear her use my full name, since I'd never told her what it was. *"Longer than it should've been,"* I replied in the same language.

She smiled. *"You didn't think I knew who you were, but I've always known. Known you were my god. Known you were the man I fell in love with as a girl."*

"I should've known I couldn't fool you." Though I hadn't realized before now, her words didn't stun me the way I thought they should. Maybe part of me had always realized too.

She met my gaze and searched my face. *"I know I don't have long, and I know I don't deserve to ask, but I have one final favor. One more prayer."*

"Anything for you."

"Please make sure Lucia is all right. Not just today, but

always. Look over her. You don't have to raise her or marry her or anything so drastic."

I pressed my lips to Fatima's forehead. "*Of course, I'll look out for my favorite niece. Always.*" When I pulled away, the brightness in Fatima's eyes was gone again, and she was staring off into space.

The exchange rang in my head, as I headed back to Lucia's car.

I was glad I'd gotten to see Fatima as herself one more time. I also hated the reminder of why I didn't dare pursue Mia.

SIX
CALEB

Most days I appreciated the silence of the library. Between students, I would sit in the private room I'd reserved for the day, and slip into a light meditation.

Today, being alone in my own head was haunting. Last night's dreams lingered, and the conversation with the stranger in the church wove its way into my thoughts.

Fortunately, my next appointment stepped into the room and greeted me with a smile, and I had something to focus on again. I was spending the day the way I did most of them, helping parish members who spoke something other than English as a first language.

Some of them needed another set of eyes on an application or resumé, and others had asked for one-on-one tutoring, outside of the classes I taught a few times a week.

Florin, my current meeting, had been a professor of social science in East Germany, forty years ago. He escaped a few years before the wall came down, and had recently decided to go back to school.

I was helping him review an essay for his college application. Languages came easily to me—one of those things I'd always been grateful for. Since I'd been given the gift, I shared it with those who needed it. For more than an hour, I sifted through Florin's paper with him, making minor tweaks and suggestions. He had it ninety-nine percent right, and was here for the reassurance as much as anything.

When we wrapped up, he shook my hand with gratitude, and I wished him luck in his interview in a few days.

Phantom pains whispered through my palm as he walked away. I wouldn't look, because there was nothing to see. The holes I remembered gouging in my own skin were a lie, because no marks lingered there now.

I left the door to my private room open again, and let the quiet, nearby conversations float toward me while I waited for the next person to arrive.

Someone was speaking in a language I didn't recognize. If I focused, I could probably make out at least a little of it, and I couldn't help but try to do exactly that. If I was hearing the conjunctions and prepositions correctly, the sentence structure was European. Did they just say *Thor*?

I strained my ears harder and caught something about a small man, or maybe it was a father, and memory. Control? There were times when new languages flowed easily for me, and this was not one of them. When the person walked away and the voice faded, I'd caught about ten percent of what they said.

And my next appointment was here.

By the time I wrapped up my day, a few hours later, I was mentally exhausted. Perfect. The walk home would tire me out physically, too, and I could shut off my brain and body for the rest of the afternoon and evening.

I was surprised to walk into the comic shop and find Teddy working instead of Mia. He was usually gone by two or three so he could spend the afternoon with his kids, and the clock behind the register said it was after four.

I didn't mind seeing him—he was a nice enough guy—but the whisper of disappointment inside made it impossible to ignore that I'd hoped to talk to Mia. For no other reason than I liked seeing her.

"Where's the boss?" I asked.

"She said she was taking the day for admin work, someplace she could concentrate," Teddy said.

Good for her, but bummer for me. It was clear she didn't want a reformed bad boy, she wanted a very-much-still-a-bad-boy—there was no question given the way she looked at Thac—but that didn't stop me from wanting her and taking every opportunity to spend time with her.

Not that I blamed her. He was muscular, tattooed, and brutal. The kind of guy who would pin me to a wall and hurt me once I'd begged enough, then follow the sting with tender kisses.

It wasn't that I denied my bisexuality. I still probably spent too much time fantasizing about Thac taking me roughly, or about myself being with Mia. Both of us with Mia.

"I hate to ask, man." Teddy grabbed his coat and pulled it on. "I thought she'd be back by now, though. I promised the girls I'd play Mario with them when they finished their homework, and they're going to be bummed if they don't have me there to kick my ass."

Thank Christ for the interruption. "No worries. I'll watch the place until she gets back. Go. Play. Have fun."

Teddy gave me a list of things I needed to know. As he left, I texted Mia to let her know about the change of plans.

Teddy had to run so I took over.

Movies tonight?

Hope you're all right.

I wasn't sure where my last message came from—it wasn't unusual for her to do this. Though if she knew Teddy had to take off at a certain time, it was a little strange for her to not be back by now.

Strange, but not unheard of.

I was grateful for the new task. For the chance to keep my mind occupied some more. I'd pick up a comic and read if I didn't need to keep my attention on the store.

The hinges on the front door squeaked and the bell chimed. Speaking of keeping bu—

It was Thac. The scowl he gave me, followed by, "Where's Mia?" didn't do anything to mute my fantasies.

"She's off-site, working on admin stuff." I knew the guy. I didn't have a problem telling him the same thing I'd been told.

"Off-site where?"

"Don't know. I don't make her tell me every single place she's going. Do you?"

His answer was a growl.

And now I knew that was a thing attractive, overbearing men actually did. *Thank Christ* I hadn't gone my entire life without that knowledge.

If I ran into this guy in an actual fight, how long could I hold my own?

Great. Now my self-destructive thoughts had moved from filthy to possibly lethal. I'd definitely last longer than he expected, though.

The silence stretching between us was awkward at best.

"Do you want me to tell her you stopped by?" I asked.

Thac stepped closer to the counter. "Actually, I'm

here to take some pictures." He held up a camera that looked like it had been around since the 1960s.

"Why?" I asked.

He shrugged. "Insurance purposes." He began to snap photos without waiting for my response.

I watched for a few seconds as pieces slotted together in my head. He took as many photos of the register area where I stood as he did anywhere else, and my suspicion grew. "Why?" I asked again. "Ronan doesn't own the property, Mia does."

Thac paused and studied me with a furrowed brow. "Then maybe I'm just here to learn about you."

"Nice deflection." I didn't buy it for a minute. "Why?" Because asking that the first two times had gotten me so much information. Still, if I kept up with the insistence he tell me something other than a lie, he might either stop with the bullshit or go away.

Did I want him to leave? He was rocking the silver-fox look, with thick, messy hair that contrasted sharply against deeply tanned skin, and a suit that was cut exquisitely for his muscular build. He was also disconcerting as fuck to spend time with.

"You're obviously more than you seem to be." Thac put away the camera and crossed his arms, then studied me more intently. He could've competed for stillness with any of the cardboard-cut-out celebrities around the room.

"I'm not anything interesting." My past was fractured, but who I currently presented myself as was the real me. Aside from the filthy fantasies. "Are you? More than you seem?"

"Without question."

A chill passed over me and crawled under my skin. Whatever the feeling was, I didn't want it here.

Thac raised an eyebrow, and leaned in resting his hands on the glass counter between us. Mia would hate that, because he was leaving fingerprints. He studied me with an intensity that felt like he thought he could pry my soul open with his gaze. "Who are you?" he asked.

If he was trying to intimidate me, it wasn't working.

"Caleb Smith. Would you like my rank, too? Not sure I have one of those. Is this an interrogation?"

"If it were, would I get the answers I want?"

"What fucking answers?" I had no idea what was going on. "I'll answer any of your questions honestly, but I don't know if I'll say what you want to hear." The crawling sensation under my skin grew, the longer he stared at me. I flexed my fingers in an attempt to ignore the feeling of claws, pushing through the skin. A familiar-but-not pressure nudged my shoulder blades. My tailbone.

"Where do you come from?" Thac asked.

"New Jersey, by way of a basket left on a doorstep." Not literally. I'd been found on the street, like an abandoned kitten, but the other explanation was one that more people connected with.

"Then you don't know where you're from."

I stared at him, hoping to convey my confusion and disbelief where my words had failed to. "I'm an orphan, so no. I don't know what your problem is, but I think you should leave until Mia gets back." The wash of darkness grew inside, and protectiveness for her mingled with rage. Irritation.

The feelings were familiar. These days, I tried to ignore things like that, but the anxious feeling that came with them, the sensation of my skin shifting and changing, was new.

Thac continued to search my face. When did this conversation go off the rails? Would I have to fight him?

Everything was culminating in a lack of control, and I hated that feeling more than anything.

Thac finally pulled his gaze from me and grabbed a nearby comic from a rack. "You're right. She's the only reason I'm here. I'll wait for her."

What about the photos? Insurance? What the fuck was going on? Asking hadn't helped. *I said* leave *now.* The roar in my head was nearly deafening. It was my voice, but from my past. That wasn't me anymore. I settled onto the bench behind the register again. My prayers had been answered, and now I had something to distract me from this morning.

Yay?

I didn't dare take my attention off him for long, because his behavior was out of place from the few interactions we'd had in the past. He glanced at me occasionally, but mostly just read the comic.

Outside, a raven cawed.

Another chill spread through me, so potent, I nearly vomited. The pain that flooded me matched what I'd dreamed about this morning, but I was pretty sure I was still awake.

I felt detached from my body and hyper aware of it at the same time. Rage flashed behind my eyelids, carried on waves of hatred. I needed to destroy *something*. The desire clawed at my hands. My shoulders. My lower back.

There was a voice on the other side of the pain. Thac? He wasn't speaking English. *Fuck,* this hurt so much.

I gripped the edge of my stool, to keep from falling off. Flames erupted from my hands?

What? I opened my mouth to speak—to scream—and a wordless roar tore from my throat.

Thac was next to me with a fire extinguisher, putting out the chair and the carpet around my feet.

Mia was going to be so pissed.

The thought was such a normal one, floating in the sea of chaos, and I picked it to focus on. To anchor myself, so I could force this feeling aside. Pain and rage ebbed, and I was in the comic shop again. The acrid smell of smoke clung to my nostrils, and the immediate space around me was ash, exposing the concrete floor underneath, but nothing else looked hurt.

Thac was watching me with a contorted expression that matched the feelings I'd just suppressed.

In a blink, his hand was on my throat. He backed me into the nearest wall. This was like a twisted fantasy, and I was instantly hard.

How fucked up was I?

Thac leaned in, until his hot breath teased my skin. "I'll ask you again, and you'll tell me the truth this time." The waves of threat that rolled from him were tangible. "What. Are. You?"

What was he looking for? What happened?

I could be flippant, but I needed answers as badly as he seemed to want them, and my confidence was gone. "I don't know."

SEVEN
MIA

I HAD MY HEAD DOWN ALL DAY, AS I WORKED ON MY finances for the next few months in an isolated corner of the library. I handled all the money stuff myself, because Dad always told me very few people could be trusted with that kind of thing.

By the time I figured out his reasons for feeling that way weren't always legal, the lesson had become a part of who I was.

When I wandered out of the library after eight, it had been dark for hours. I hadn't meant to spend the entire day there, which meant I'd missed lunch. My stomach growled with displeasure.

Maybe Caleb wanted to keep me company for dinner. I grabbed my phone.

Missed calls. Missed texts.

Oops.

There was a text from Teddy, and then a voicemail, both asking if I was going to be back soon because he had to go. A short while later, there was another text from Caleb letting me know he'd taken over the shop for the night and sent Teddy home.

I sent Teddy a message first, apologizing and telling him I owed him and that I'd make it up to him. Then I called Caleb.

No answer.

So I sent him a text too. *Bringing home food. Tell me what you want.*

I started the walk home. The chill cut into my face, and the traffic was heavy as people rushed home. But it was a good chance to reset my brain after a day of numbers.

As I passed by the Indian place a few blocks from home, Caleb hadn't replied yet. He must be busy—no big deal. My next message to him said, *Hope you're in the mood for curry and naan.*

A short while later, I neared my shop, food in hand and making my stomach protest that it had to wait any longer for a taste.

The lights were on inside the store, but the *Closed* sign was on the door. Thac was visible through the glass.

Maybe he was why Caleb wasn't answering. They didn't get along, but I was happy to see Thac two days in a row. If I invited him to stay, would things be tense, or could I actually make them be friends?

I pushed inside the shop, and the heavy smell of smoke hit me. "What happened?" Already scanning the room, I set my stuff on the nearest clean space. I saw hints of fire damage behind the register but nowhere else. As I got closer, I also saw the remnants of white foam and the shop fire extinguisher and a few square feet of ruined carpet.

"Did one of you light my store on fire?" I looked between them. Why hadn't either man given me an answer yet?

"It was a small accident." Thac spoke first, with the kind of confidence that said he expected me to accept his answer and be okay with it.

I wasn't. "I'm glad it wasn't on purpose. What were you doing?"

"I had a loose thread on my sweater." Caleb tugged at the sleeve. "Thac was melting it for me so it wouldn't unravel."

Thac groaned softly.

I stared at Caleb trying to convey my disbelief. "Uh-huh. The entire area behind the register is destroyed. I'm going to have to bring someone in to replace that carpet."

"We were about to clean it up," Thac said. "I'll take care of replacing it. Don't you worry about it."

Excuse me? "I am worried about it, because there was a fire. What were you doing?"

"He's right. We'll clean it up. We were about to do

that anyway." Caleb's tone was as dismissive as Thac's.

I was calling bullshit. On all of it—whatever secret the men were keeping, thinking they could make me ignore this, trying to brush me off.

Did Valkyries have to deal with this kind of bullshit?

Damn it, why did I have to think that? "No. You're not going to clean it up, because you're not telling me what happened. You can fess up, or you can leave so I can pick up your mess."

"Mia, please." Caleb's tone wasn't pleading, despite the words.

"We'll take care of it." Thac sounded firm as well.

I sighed. "What happened?"

"He had a loose thread—"

"Nope." I cut Thac off. "Both of you go." Because I was about two-point-five seconds from losing my shit.

Thac opened his mouth, as if to protest.

"Now," I barked.

They both walked out the door, scowls on their faces.

I could freak out later. Right now I had work to do. The list was already ticking off in my head.

Learn how to clean up the mess from a fire extinguisher.

Call someone to replace the carpet.

Tell Teddy the shop was closed for the next couple of days but that I'd pay him for the time anyway.

Figure out how I was going to pay for all of this without touching my trust fund.

The rest I'd deal with when I got there.

Seriously, what the hell were Caleb and Thac thinking? Doing? I wanted that answer even more than I wanted to know why Kirby believed I'd make a good Valkyrie.

The questions bounced in my head as I gathered the supplies I needed to clean up the mess. Fortunately, most of it was basic stuff—gloves, alcohol, baking soda. I even had the masks from the three-month stint I'd had with learning to cast resin dice.

Why did I send Kirby away?

Why was I more fixated on a bullshit offer that wasn't meant for me than I was on what my renter and my dad's enforcer had done to start a localized fire in the middle of my comic shop?

Kirby had offered me something I'd wanted for ages—the chance to be a superhero. And I turned it down because of…

What?

Insecurity.

Lack of faith.

Her offer couldn't be real. Why would she want me? I was thirty. Tall. Awkward. Not in any way athletic or powerful or strong.

But why would she approach me if it wasn't real?

Should I tell Scarlett? Should I call her?

I finished blotting and sweeping and vacuuming

as best I could, and then stepped back, to look at my work. The area behind the register was still a mess, but the chemicals were gone. Now I just needed to get rid of the smell in the air. This wasn't exactly a great time of year for airing the shop out, and I wasn't going to do it at night anyway.

Neither Thac nor Caleb had called—though to be fair I wasn't subtle about the way I told them to leave —and my untouched curry sat on the counter, cold and mocking me, as my stomach growled in response. It was after midnight; no wonder I was hungry.

My phone buzzed, and I grabbed it with both of their names flitting in my mind and asking if I was really still upset.

Yes. Seriously—what the hell had they been thinking? Doing?

It was a message from Scarlett, though. *Call me when you see this.*

She probably didn't mean now, but I needed to hear a friendly voice, so I dialed.

She answered quickly. "What are you doing up?"

"Long, messy story." I thought for a minute. "Actually, no, it's not long, but it feels like it should be. I'm cleaning up a mess, and don't ask for details because I don't have them."

"Boo." Scarlett's frown was reflected in her voice. Thank the gods for sympathetic BFFs. "Does that mean maybe you need a vacation? Scratch that, there's no maybe here. You needed a vacation anyway, and this is just more proof."

Random. "I have so much to do here."

"It's not your mess, is it? Tell the person who made it to clean it up. Here's the thing… Some of the Valkyries are going to spend the next few days here, and I was thinking you should too. No one said anything about keeping other guests out of the place while they were here, so if you just happened to be here, you could meet real life magic people."

Yesterday, that would've sounded amazing. Now it reminded me of this morning's encounter with Kirby and how I still didn't know if turning her down was the right choice. "I know you. You're magic."

"Yeah, but there will be more than me, and if you ran into them while they were here, I could introduce you."

Would that make me regret my decision even more? Probably. I did love the pictures I'd seen of Scarlett's resort, though, and I missed her, and I wouldn't be working in here for a few days. "I have to tell you something first. She approached me this morning."

"She? Who?"

"Kirby. I met her. She offered to make me into a Valkyrie." Saying the words aloud reinforced how ridiculous they were.

Silence met me. And a huff followed. "And you didn't tell me?"

"You were sleeping." Yeah, weak excuse. I leaned against the nearby counter, and plucked a steam-soggy piece of naan from my takeout.

"When did it happen? Because I'm awake now, you're awake now… Does that mean you're coming anyway? How could you not tell me? Do you love your wings?"

She thought I'd accepted.

I nibbled on my cold food. "I turned her down."

"What?"

"You heard me."

"I didn't, because you made me go deaf from disbelief. Why? Why why why?"

Great. Now she was vocalizing the day's mental exercises. "A lot of reasons. But what if I made a mistake?"

"Then this is your chance to rectify things. I'll send Pan, you'll visit for a day or two, and while you're here, you'll meet some of the others. If you love them and love the vibe, maybe you can still change your mind. And if not, you'll know for certain you were right, and you'll still get a mini vacation. Plus, I'll get to see you."

Scarlett's generosity and kindness were some of the reasons she made a great friend.

I still had concerns though. "Are you sure I'm allowed to be there while they are?"

"My hotel, my rules. You're allowed to stay here if I say so. Besides, Kirby didn't take issue with it when I asked her. I wish she'd told me why not. I wish you had."

"I know. I'm sorry. But also, it's late, I'm tired, and I'm gross."

Scarlett huffed again. "If you don't want to come, just say so."

"I do, though."

"It's settled, then. Pack a bag, and Pan will be there in ten minutes. You can take a bath here, sleep as long as you want, and then meet everyone."

I shouldn't. It was irresponsible to run off.

But I wasn't *running off;* I was going on vacation, like Scarlett said. "Okay. Ten minutes. Pan had better be here."

"He will be."

I was actually a little giddy as I locked up the store and headed back to my house. I didn't want to toss a whole thing of curry out, but I also didn't want to come home to the smell in my fridge. Maybe those ravens would come along and enjoy it if I left it on top of the trash. Did they eat things like that?

Who knew?

While I got ready, I sent Teddy a quick note asking if he'd be here for the carpet guy. I left Caleb a note on the table telling him I'd be gone for a few days. Should I tell Thac?

No. I didn't check in with him like he was some

sort of babysitter, and he was being weird hanging around and not telling me why. Besides, he knew about the fire, and he wasn't giving me details. He could worry for a day or so. He'd better worry.

I was ready when Pan knocked on my door. Scarlett was so lucky—a fucking god loved her. How cool was that?

I locked the house up, and he took my hand. The trip itself was disorienting. One minute we were in my place, and then we were in Scarlett's hotel in Greece.

That was it. No weird, stretching feeling or any other number of things that the movies alluded to. Just blink—new room. Having Pan and Scarlett appear in my shop was one thing, but traveling this way myself made it all so much more real.

"Scarlett sends her apologies." Pan handed me a key and a room number. "She got called away by a guest, right after she spoke to you. She says to go take care of yourself, and call her when you're done or after you've slept."

I realized we were standing in front of the room that matched the number on my key.

"Okay. Thank you." I let myself into the room, and the peaceful ambiance sank in. The floor was a medium hardwood, stretching out to a balcony that looked over some of the most vibrant green I'd ever seen. The blue of the sky sparkled down on me through glass, even from here. And the bed, draped in muted linens, beckoned me as exhaustion filled my bones.

What was happening to my world?

EIGHT
CALEB

What was going on? One minute, Mister Tall-Dark-and-Fuckable was threatening me, and the next, my ass and feet were on fire.

My skin hadn't burned, though, and neither had anything I was wearing.

I had no idea what to tell Mia because I didn't understand what had happened. She kicked us out, and before I could figure out what I was doing, Thac grabbed my arm and yanked me through a doorway less than a block from Mia's shop.

We were in an apartment. I'd take the time to appreciate the beauty, but I had other things on my mind.

Thac finally let me go.

That didn't de-escalate anything in my mind.

"If you don't know what you are, you're dangerous," he said.

Dude needed to learn a new tune. "Why are you so obsessed with what I am?"

"Because in Mia's shop, you started to take on non-human features."

"What? Are you high?" Was I high? Did he drug me? I hadn't had anything to drink or eat since he showed up. Was this low blood sugar? My gaze landed on what looked like a window at the far end of the apartment, and the view made my brain twitch. "Why do you have a fake window with a picture of St. Louis?" I wandered toward the image that looked more and more real the closer I got.

Down to the people walking and the cars driving on the street below.

"It's not fake," Thac said. "We're in St. Louis."

Where Mia had grown up. Where her father still lived. What. The actual. Fuck? "Are you going to hand me over to him?"

"You're not very bright, are you?" That was what Thac said, but those weren't the sounds that came out of his mouth. He was speaking in a language I'd never heard before an hour or two ago. How did I know what he said?

No clue. *"Bright enough to understand you,"* I replied in the same language, and somehow managed to hide my surprise that I could.

Thac's shock shone through. "You speak the ancient tongue? Since when?"

Ancient tongue? Like we were in some sort of

RPG? "Since now." The flippant answer would probably get me punished, but telling him the truth had as well, and if he went back to manhandling me, maybe I could focus on desire instead of this cloying confusion.

He stared at me for a few seconds that felt like an eternity, then frowned. "I'm not going to hand you over to Ronan, no. I brought you to my place because you're not human. If you're lying about not knowing, that's dangerous. If you truly don't know, that's even more dangerous."

"Of course I'm human." I made a show of patting the top of my head. My ass. "Did I grow kitty ears? A puppy tail. Oh no," I feigned dismay. "Did I wag my tail when you were choking me? How. Embarrassing." There was still the matter of that whole fire thing, but there was an explanation for that. People didn't just randomly burst into flames. Didn't MythBusters prove that?

Or was he talking about something else? He'd pushed me for an answer before the whole fire thing. I racked my brain. "Is this about when I saved Mia from—" I snapped my jaw shut when confusion bled into Thac's expression.

"When you what?" Damn his growl was sexier than it had the right to be.

"You didn't know? It was ages ago. Forget I said anything." *And don't think for a minute you can get mad at Mia for keeping the secret.*

"You really don't know," Thac said.

One track mind, this one. "You think? What gave me away? *Maybe I'm not the one who's not so bright.*" I spoke the last sentence in this new ancient language I apparently knew. "How about, since you think you know what's going on, you tell me? Start with why you claim we're in St. Louis."

"Because we are. We came here through a fae gate."

Nutso alert.

Except that his words rang more true than I wanted them to. Not only because Thac didn't strike me as the kind of guy with a sense of humor, but also because part of me believed him. Knew what he was saying was true, as easily as I knew how to speak a language I'd never heard before. "Fae, like faeries?"

"Yes."

I wouldn't believe him. I couldn't believe him. "That's it. I'm out." I strolled toward the front door.

A gust of wind struck me in the chest and pushed me back until my ass landed on the couch.

"You're not leaving until we're done talking," Thac's voice was a low rumble, humming through the floor.

"Are you holding me prisoner?" This should be hot, right?

Thac gave a single, curt nod. "Until we figure out who you are. You nearly burned Mia's shop down, you hold impressive magics, and you don't even know magic is real. How can I let you leave?"

I didn't have an answer. My brain was too busy warring with itself over whether he was insane, or I was for believing him. "I'm not magic."

"Fire came out of your hands."

"Are you magic?" *Way to deflect, me.*

"I am a god."

Yeah you are, big guy. How do you want me to worship you? "Okay. Keep telling yourself that."

Thac narrowed his eyes, raised one hand, and snapped his fingers.

Thunder cracked near my head, making me jump, and rain started to fall. Only on me. And it evaporated before it hit the sofa, leaving my hair and shirt drenched, but everything around me dry.

The conversation I'd overheard in the library slammed back into my thoughts. "Holy… Are you Thor?"

"Take his asinine name out of your infantile mouth." Thac sounded disgusted.

Okay then. "Um… I'm sorry. I can't wrap my brain around this." But I could. I didn't want to, but I was looking directly at proof of what he was saying. At least some of it. How could I deny what I saw with my own eyes? What I'd known for so long? The knowledge of this truth rang deep in my core.

"Let's say I believe you." I felt both idiotic and relieved to speak the words aloud. "Can you help me figure out what I am? It's not like I know anyone else to ask."

"That's not what I do."

Wait. All of this insistence and questioning and kidnapping and he wasn't going to help? "You just said you're going to keep me here until I figure things out. You've signed yourself up for the job."

"You won't like my methods." More menace slipped into his voice.

Because apparently that was possible. And also, what the fuck was wrong with me that it turned me on?

The same things that had always been wrong with me, but tonight, I might not have the strength to fight them. "Why not?"

"If I help you learn, I will tear down your restraints, to do so. Any self-control you have, any walls you've put up, will vanish, to get your mind to stop rejecting what your body knows."

Like that, I was rock hard. Fantasizing about what he meant. Picturing this large, scary man with the sexy as hell tattoos making me lose my inhibitions. "Yeah, let's skip that." Most difficult thing I'd said tonight.

"I'll put in some calls to some people, but I have to wait until I hear back from them." Thac pulled his phone from his jacket pocket. "Stay."

"Yes sir." The words came out without thought, and I hid a wince.

Magic. Not like God's blessings, but like rain, coming out of nowhere in the middle of a building, because a guy snapped his fingers.

Did Mia know? She couldn't. Did her father have any idea who was working for him? Why did a god work for a crime lord?

Why was a god madly in lust with the woman I rented a room from? I mean, aside from the obvious, that she was hot and fun and—

"I've left some messages." Thac returned more quickly than I expected. "We have to wait until someone calls me back."

Here? In this comfortable apartment with him?

Oh damn. "Great. We'll sit here and watch TV until one of your friends gets back to you." Conversation was a bad idea. He'd do more of that growling thing, I'd do more of that being-turned-on thing, and the entire evening would be uncomfortable. More uncomfortable. "Do you have a TV?"

"I do." Thac dropped into a nearby chair and grabbed a remote from a spot I hadn't seen, under the coffee table. He pressed a button, and a panel in the far wall slid open, revealing a TV that was so big it shouldn't be legal.

So the man had at least one vice besides watching Mia. What else did he like to watch?

The TV flipped on, and instead of a screen full of a couple-dozen recommended TV shows and channels, we were looking at a load screen for a movie.

Correction—an MMA fight. Thac didn't ask if I was okay with the choice, he just pressed Play.

I might not be familiar with his vices, but I was intensely aware of my own, and I was about to be so fucked.

The first couple of matches, the fighters went to the mat quickly and spent most of their time grappling. Their technique was sloppy, their moves not-quite polished. Not that I could take either one of them now, but a few years ago, I would've had them tapping- or choked-out in a couple of minutes.

The third fight though—the kicks, the punches, and the more subtle attacks that would leave hidden bruises for weeks—crawled under my skin and dragged up the past. The need to either inflict or receive the agony. The rush that always lingered after a match. The drive that came with it to feel more. To suffer more.

But I'd moved past thinking I needed that in my life.

The fight was over, and my curiosity wouldn't be distracted any longer. I wanted to know more about this world that existed all around me, that I'd never seen. "Is this what a god's life is always like? Flirt with sexy humans. Kidnap the people who live with them. Watch a fight on TV and go to bed?" So many people would be disappointed with that reality.

"What would you rather I be doing?" Thac asked.

"I don't know. You can make it rain indoors.

Shouldn't you be answering prayers, or dishing out punishment and reward or something?"

"Does your god do that?" The way he raised his eyebrows made me feel like I'd asked a foolish question.

If he did, I might still believe in him. "I don't have a god."

"Hmm…" Thac's look shifted from condescending to penetrating, as he studied me.

I wouldn't take the bait and ask what the grunt meant.

"A prayer isn't like wishing on a star or blowing out the candles on a birthday cake," he said. "It's not a list for Santa. I hear the heart's desire of those who worship me either by name or with their actions. Most of that sounds like whispers on the wind, though sometimes, it's a shout or a cry. Rarely is it possible or wise for me to act, in those few instances where I understand the words."

"Really." That sounded like a weak excuse.

"I'm not omnipotent. If a grandfather in Argentina calls my name, begs me to save their grandchild, and offers his own life in exchange, I feel his pain. I feel his sincerity. I don't have the power to act. I can bless someone with prosperity or famine, but I can't grant life."

When he put it that way… I wanted to argue but I couldn't find flaw in his reply. "That kind of sucks."

Thac gave me a wry smile. "It's vexing at times.

It's heartbreaking at times. After more than a thousand years, I've learned to accept that I continue to live when others don't. That doesn't mean I'm immune to their pain."

The words and sentiment behind them were profound. It almost felt disrespectful that part of me also thought it was sexy that he felt that way. "So you're telling me even being a god doesn't solve all a person's problems."

"It might solve some people's. It comes with many of its own. For instance, I still had to make reservations to get those Rocky Horror tickets for Mia."

Was that humor? "Did you just crack a joke?"

"I'm not emotionless."

"Only toward me?" I asked.

"Not even toward you. You would be nothing if you didn't know Mia. Or, you might have been until fire came out of your hands when you were scared."

"Pissed off. I wasn't scared." Okay, so I'd been a little terrified back in Mia's shop. "I'd be nothing? Really?"

Thac raised his brows. "If I met you in a club, I'd bring you home and fuck you."

So gods went clubbing. Not where my mind wanted to go, but if I let it travel on its own, it would plummet into the gutter, where a large, powerful man taught me how an immortal screwed.

"And then drain my life energy and make me

your immortal servant?" I needed the dark humor, to distract myself.

"You watch too many movies. I'm not a metamoura."

I didn't know what that meant, but it sounded terrifying. "If I were to say yes to your methods to discover what I am, what would be involved?" I didn't mean to ask that. Not out loud. But my defenses were low anyway, and now the question was out there.

He paused the fight. "If you've suppressed your powers, your subconscious wants to protect you. I incite, and we see how you react."

First of all, this was an odd time in my life for my body to choose that path, and second, I was pretty sure I'd seen that movie—torture caused my secret mutant cells to try to protect me. "Deadpool style?"

"I don't intend to kill you. Mia would be upset."

Not comforting. "Not what I meant."

"There's no pain involved in this," Thac said. "At least not physical. Your mind may object. But I essentially weave a series of spells around you, to make your mind release what it's holding onto. It's like being drunk or high but more controlled. Magical instead of chemical."

That didn't sound so bad. Not that I liked the idea of losing control, but I knew who I was, and I didn't have anything to hide. "If I tell you I'm fine with that

—if I give you some sort of explicit permission—will you just do it and get it over with?"

He studied me for a moment, brow furrowed. "Yes."

"Great. You have my permission." Maybe I could go home and sleep in my own bed tonight.

"Follow me." Without waiting, Thac turned and strode toward the counter that separated the kitchen from the living room. He pulled out a stool, and pointed. "Sit."

I scrambled to obey, while trying to look casual, and perched on the new seat.

"Shirt off," he said.

Yes sir. Nope. Wasn't letting another one of those out. I stripped off my sweater, and unbuttoned my shirt, then folded both and set them on the stool next to me.

He stood behind me, and a silence settled into the room. With his first light touch—a barely-there whisper of skin on skin, I sucked in a sharp breath through my teeth.

I forced myself to rein in the reaction, and focused on relaxing. Finding that center that usually calmed me, but had eluded me the last few days.

The longer he worked, the easier it was to drift toward that place. Finally, tension sapped from my body. My mind loosened. Peace settled in.

With all of the anxiousness gone, I was free to enjoy how good his fingers felt tracing patterns along my back. There was a peace in this. A fresh kind of desire.

He'd said something about my losing my inhibitions, but this was just calm. It was incredible.

And so was Thac. Whatever he was doing to me hummed with delicious allure over my entire body. It was like being wrapped in silk and floating away.

Or being wrapped in him. It was easy to close my eyes and picture it. Feel it. His strong, firm body pinning me down. Embracing me. Penetrating me.

As he dipped toward my waist, my desire spiked. He drew a line up my spine, and the intensity of my want didn't lessen.

This was incredible.

This was what I wanted but couldn't have.

Why not? I was right here. He was right here. Why was I denying myself?

Mia likes him.

As she should.

She'd be hurt.

She could join us next time. Any weak, whimpering argument that flitted out from the back of my mind was easily squashed. There was no reason to worry about any of it.

If I reached just a little deeper, would I touch what I was looking for? Would I find what he was looking for?

Did I care?

I spun on the stool, and Thac took a step back, his eyes wide.

"Don't go." I was on my feet in a blink, pressing my body to his. I draped my arms around his neck. "We're having so much fun, and we're about to have even more."

NINE
THAC

Mia's renter was throwing himself at me. He had that slender-but-muscular frame pressed against mine, and his desire pressed into my thigh through our jeans.

She'd be so upset if I fucked him.

He might be as well, regardless of what he thought at this moment. He was currently the magical equivalent of drunk.

It took more restraint than I expected, to reach up and unhook his arms from their lock around me. "You need to sleep off this process." I hadn't unlocked any latent magic in him anyway.

Caleb jutted out his lower lip. "I'm not sleepy. Unless this is your way of getting me into your bed."

"Quite literally, yes." I led him into the bedroom.

He looked disappointed when I didn't join him in bed, but within a few seconds of lying down, he closed his eyes, and his breathing changed. He was asleep.

His behavior and his exhaustion meant my magic did what I intended it to, but it hadn't had the desired results. Damn.

As I turned away, a flash of color caught my eye, and I spun back to look at Caleb. Wings had sprouted from his back—leathery and lizard-like, in iridescent white with traces of fuchsia and a deep, violent red. A tail peeked above pants that were drooping on his hips as he slept, and it almost looked like scales covered portions of his back and arms.

A dragon?

That was impossible, but I was definitely looking at something that fit the description. How didn't he know that he had this kind of power?

I spent the next few hours watching Caleb sleep, with Mia's voice taunting me. *Kind of creepy, don't you think?*

I didn't dare let him out of my sight until he was back to his restrained self. Not that I minded the scenery. With the random pattern of scales and flesh covering his body, and his clothes pulling up to expose hints of muscle and strength, he made for a fascinating and tempting view.

He'd been intriguing before. Desirable. This, however, raised the bar of temptation quite a bit higher. Not just because of the power that lay under his skin, but also because of the man he was. The questions he'd asked. The way he saw the world.

Add his potential immortality to that…

He was most certainly as appealing as he was compelling.

As Caleb stirred, I tensed. With his groan, his wings vanished as if they'd never been there, and as he sat up, his tail disappeared as well.

The threat was tucked away again, but for how long?

He focused on me. "How long have you been here?"

"Since you passed out a few hours ago." I saw no reason to hide it. "How much do you remember?"

Caleb furrowed his brow, then let out another groan and pressed his hand to his forehead. "I'm still dressed, which means it's unlikely anything happened beyond what I remember so… all of it? Fuck. I feel hungover."

"That is a side effect, yes. A consequence of your mind's letting go of everything, then rapidly trying to rebuild what it lost." I was sympathetic. What I put him through wasn't the greatest sensation, and the psychological consequences impacted most beings the same, regardless of whether they healed quickly or not.

"Kinda wish you'd told me that before we started."

"I apologize. Would it have changed your answer?"

"No."

My phone rang from the other room. "I'll be back." I went to see who was calling. Ronan's name flashed on the screen.

"Evening, old friend," I answered with my typical greeting.

"Evening." Stress ran through the single word. "I'm sorry to call during your downtime, I need you here, though."

That didn't sound great. "I'll be there in five."

I didn't have to ask where *here* was. Ronan's office was at the top of the skyscraper a few buildings down from my apartment building. He owned the entire tower, and had offered me a room there more than once. He preferred to be high above the city, to keep himself away from the glut of energy that radiated from so many different beings.

On the other hand, I preferred to stay close to the earth. To feel what lay under the city.

I didn't want to leave Caleb alone, but he was alert and probably wouldn't change while I was gone. It was unlikely Ronan would need me for long.

If I could take a picture of Caleb in this form, they would definitely expose something to the right eye, but it felt awkward to ask.

What was wrong with me that I cared?

I returned to my bedroom.

"We're done. I can go home now?" Caleb asked.

Absolutely not. "I'm still not letting you loose on Mia's world until we have answers about your random bursts of magic."

"So I'm your prisoner?"

"I suppose."

"Not nearly as sexy as the fantasies."

I glowered. "I need to go to a meeting. I won't be gone long, but don't go anywhere."

"Yeah. Okay. What's to stop me from walking out right now? Or calling the police. Or… anything else?"

If Caleb was a dragon, he could shatter any spell I put in place to keep him here. I still doubted he was, and he didn't have that kind of control.

But I'd rather he not try.

Besides, there were only three dragons in existence, there had only ever been three dragons, and Caleb was not one of them.

"I'm not doing this to be cruel," I said. "This is for your safety as well. Stay, so you can have answers."

He seemed to consider this. "Fine. But I'm using your shower while you're gone."

"Make yourself at home." I gestured broadly. "I'll be back."

I strolled the short distance to Ronan's building, and gave a terse nod to the doorman, an argus whose dozens of eyes were magical rather than physical, and scanned the magical signatures of everyone who entered. Between him and the elevator, there were at least half-a-dozen more magical beings who looked harmless, but could maim or kill with a thought or a flick of their wrist.

All of them were loyal to Ronan, because he'd saved them and given them a new life.

Though he didn't run the top-secret crime ring that Mia thought he did, Ronan still needed a certain level of ruthlessness. It kept those same people in the lobby, along with their families and dozens of others, safe. It was what kept Ronan and Mia safe.

The elevator carried me up to the top floor, only because it recognized my thumbprint. It was amazing how magic and technology could frequently look and act so similar. I stepped out of the box and into an office that spread out in front of me, a large portion partitioned off as Ronan's office.

He was seated at his desk, but stood with a tight smile the instant he saw me, and watched me approach. Looking at him, it was clear where Mia got some of her looks—her stunning eyes and thick, dark hair, her strong stance and the attitude she radiated.

Most of his furnishings were made of wood but didn't look like traditional furniture. The designs had a more organic flow, as if trees and other plants had grown into a chair or table shape, and then surrendered their offering, in exchange for the gift of continuing to live and grow.

The photograph of Mia's mother on his desk could've been a snapshot in time of Mia the day I met her. Though her mother had jet black hair and pale, freckled skin, her face was Mia's. Her smile was Mia's. There were so many ways it was obvious how much and why Ronan adored his daughter.

Though he never talked about his late wife, I knew losing her had nearly destroyed him. He'd surrendered his fae birthright to be with her, and loved her more than anything. He treated Mia like his most precious possession now that her mother was gone.

We exchanged terse, brief greetings. Ronan didn't offer me a seat, and I didn't try to take one. This didn't strike me as being that sort of meeting.

Instead, I stood on one side of a desk with twisty legs, the top portion of a tree supporting a flat surface, and he settled into a chair across from me. Though he no longer lived among the fae, their rules and traditions were ingrained in him, and we observed a lot of those polite formalities in his presence.

"What can I do for you?" I got right to the point. Yes, we were friends. Equals. Off the clock, Ronan and I drank together, laughed together, and relived old stories together. In here, he was king. And in this setting, in his realm, I deferred to him. As he would to me if we were in my domain.

Though, I had no interest in leading. My joy was in punishment and reward.

"I understand you went to see Mia yesterday," he said.

I raised an eyebrow and let my unspoken question

of *have you been watching me* linger between us. "I did."

"And?"

I was expected to explain why. *I missed those incredible curves and her musical laugh* wasn't the right answer. "The magics around her are clashing with the wards. I'm trying to determine what's causing it without alerting her."

A few of the lines faded from Ronan's forehead, and some of the tension drained from his neck, though not enough for him to relax in his seat. "I have similar concerns. Something's wrong. Any hints on your side?"

"I don't know yet, beyond disruption and an unsettling feeling." I wasn't ready to give up the information about Caleb. If I was wrong, and Ronan acted on it, Mia would be furious that her friend was hurt.

"I know this goes without saying, but today, your agreement must be explicit. What I'm about to tell you *cannot* go beyond this room. It stays between you and me." Ronan spoke with severity.

Intriguing and concerning. "Of course."

He held out both hands, one palm up and the other with his index finger extended. His fingernail grew into a long, sharp claw, and he sliced along his exposed skin, leaving a swell of blood. "Your word."

A blood oath? To talk about Mia? This was an unbreakable bond until he and I agreed to end it.

What was coming for her? I extended my hand without hesitation, and he cut me as well, so we could shake hands.

"Whatever is said next in this room only stays between us," I agreed. "You have my promise."

Ronan waved a hand, and the air around us changed. The pressure and the magic in the room changed, like a shift in the sky right before a storm. I recognized the feeling—he'd isolated us from the rest of the human realm. Moved us to a pocket of the fae realm instead.

That was a dangerous place for him to visit under normal circumstances, and spoke to the severity of the situation as much as the blood oath did. We were mostly safe for a short while though, as he'd done the equivalent of hiding us in the corner of a dark closet.

No one would find us or be able to hear us.

What was going on?

"Odin is back." Ronan spoke to my curiosity and amplified my concern in a blink.

Odin was an old god who was supposedly destroyed centuries ago. A being who wreaked havoc on even his own followers.

Not the kind of god that man or magical being needed to return to the living.

"Or rather, he was apparently never gone." Ronan continued before I could speak. "He's spent centuries in a weakened state, hiding, and that time has changed him. He's not the same god we once knew. He's kinder. More reasonable."

I had a hard time believing that, but Ronan wasn't an easy man to convince that someone had changed. I didn't understand why we cared. Fae and elves didn't deal in the affairs of gods. I didn't deal in the affairs of the European gods—they tended to be brutal and territorial.

There were a handful of them—Freyr and Fenrir in Chicago, Freya, and a few of the Celtic gods—who had the same *live and let live* mindset I did, but most of the others were brutal and narcissistic.

I didn't want to ask my next question, but I had to. "How can you be certain he's a different man? Gods don't change. They're literally made up of the faith that created them."

"You changed."

"No. I'm still the same at my core, I just express it differently."

Ronan sighed. "Extreme circumstances change everyone. Odin is not the same god anyone knew."

If Ronan said it was true, then I would trust him. "What does this have to do with Mia?"

"Odin cursed a Valkyrie, centuries ago."

I was familiar with the story, as were most immortals. If for no other reason than the men who loved her had spent centuries tearing across various lands to find her in her reincarnated forms.

If I'd been tense before, it was nothing compared

to what coiled through me now. "I know Kirby's story."

"She's alive again." Ronan's news wasn't surprising. Part of Odin's curse was that she would be reincarnated again and again. "But this time she has the power to make more."

"Make more... Valkyries?" I didn't know how to feel about that.

Ronan gave a terse nod. "She's raising an army, and she's going to use them to hunt gods. She's become a killer in this life."

"Valkyries don't kill; they ferry the dead to Valhalla." Nothing about this sounded right.

Ronan stood and came around to my side of the desk. He leaned against the sturdy furniture and studied me. "This one kills." He pulled out his phone and flipped through a series of images. I recognized the woman, but the activities looked out of an over-hyped action movie. She was wielding heavy, very human weapons. Following human targets.

Though none of the images were executions, killing was implied in more than one. "How did you get these?" I asked.

Ronan set his phone down. "She's a threat to a lot of gods. She's destroyed a lot of lives, and there are beings watching her when they can, to ensure she doesn't hurt them again."

It was difficult to deny the evidence in front of me.

"And she's making more like her." I had to repeat it to believe it.

"To try to start Ragnarök," Ronan said.

I was ambivalent about the news. Ragnarök wouldn't impact us directly; it was the death and rebirth of other pantheons, not mine. It had nothing to do with the fae or elves. But the resulting incidental damage would spread far and wide.

"What does this have to do with us?" I asked.

"Her next target to change is Mia."

My blood turned to ice in my veins. No one magical was touching Mia, especially for this.

"Keep her safe?" Ronan's words made it easier for me to do what I intended regardless. "Don't let them make my girl into a Valkyrie and keep this conversation in confidence, and I'll never ask anything of you again."

"I work for you because I want to." There was no need for me to remind him, but it felt appropriate.

Ronan nodded. "My statement—my request—stands. Don't let anything happen to her."

I wouldn't. No one who meant Mia harm would get near her, if I had to surrender everything to make it so.

Caleb would need to wait longer. I had to get Mia. It didn't matter if she protested; I wasn't leaving her alone. Not with this kind of threat out there.

A short while later, I found myself walking into her shop once again. Or trying to. The doors were locked, and the *Closed* sign was out. I hammered on the glass, barely showing enough restraint to keep from shattering it.

One of the employees answered. "Sorry. We're closed for repairs."

Because Caleb had started a fire. Because I'd driven him to… "Where's Mia?"

"She said she was going on vacation."

What? Without telling her father? Without saying anything to me? "Where?"

"I don't know, but I think you should leave, man." The guy looked nervous.

I shouldn't terrorize him. I already had one of those to deal with back home. "Yeah. Thank you."

I dialed Mia.

No answer.

Where the fuck was she, and would I have to see how much damage I could do to a Valkyrie, to keep her safe?

TEN
MIA

LAST NIGHT WAS A BLUR, BUT WAKING UP IN A BED THAT wasn't my own, in a cozy guesthouse, confirmed for me that at least part of it really happened.

As much as I wanted to believe it was only the good parts, I suspected the carpet in my shop still needed to be replaced, and Thac and Caleb really had hidden the why of it all from me.

There was a cream-colored envelope on the floor near my door, and I picked it up. I didn't see any writing on the outside, so I pulled the small note card out from inside.

Text me when you wake up, and I'll be right there. So glad you came. Scarlett.

The note made me smile. It still felt weird to walk away from work like this—to just leave it all behind for a day or two—but the change in scenery was nice, and so was the idea of hanging out with Scarlett. I texted her, told her I was going to shower and get dressed, and to let herself in.

I wanted to take my time in the shower, but I also didn't want to keep Scarlett waiting. It felt good to wash away the grime and frustration of last night's emergency cleaning binge, though.

When I emerged from the bathroom, still wringing water from my hair, I found a serving tray with breakfast on the table in the main room, and Scarlett in one of the chairs.

She pushed out the chair across from her with her foot. "Pan wasn't happy I lowered myself to serving a guest, but he made an exception for you."

"That was sweet of him." My tone was sarcastic, but not mean. She was so lucky to have guys like him and Arnlaug.

I reached the table, and Scarlett rose to pull me into a hug. "I'm so glad you came." She gave me a tight squeeze, and I returned it. "I still can't believe this whole Kirby-approaching-you thing," she said as she pulled away.

"Ridiculous, right?"

Scarlett furrowed her brows. "That you turned her down? Yes. I respect your decision, but also, you're an idiot. She wanted you for a reason."

"Is that coffee?" I dropped into my chair and grabbed the cup not in front of Scarlett's seat. Enjoying the hot drink was far better than having Scarlett chime in with what half of my brain was already saying. "Oh God, this is good. I can't get coffee like this at home."

"Pan has skills that extend beyond magic… In the bedroom and out." Scarlett gestured to the dangerously tempting spread of crepes covered with fresh berries. "Eat up."

Yummy. "I need to figure out how to get my own personal in-house barista and chef. Even a day of this and I'm going to be spoiled." I grabbed a fork. "You're helping me eat this, right?"

"I might nibble." Scarlett speared a strawberry. "You could come live in the hotel, and then you'd have all of that."

I wasn't sure our career paths overlapped like that.

Especially with her being one of the future saviors of the world and all that.

I was going to be seeing reminders all day of the Valkyries. Of what I'd been offered and turned down. I stood by my observation that Kirby was wrong about me, but it would take a little while for me to convince the comic-loving-little-girl part of me of that.

Being here would hurt, but it should also be fun, and I'd get over the bad bits. "What's on the agenda?"

"Kirby wanted to plan the entire day, down to the minute." Scarlett sipped her coffee. "A few of us convinced her that wasn't as much fun, and now we're playing it by ear. Mostly, we're here to have fun."

That sounded… well… fun. "A few of you? How many people are here?"

"About ten or eleven women, including you and me."

Oh. "I don't know if I expected more or less." An army was huge, wasn't it? Though armies of magical beings were probably different. Unless they were fighting other magical beings? Did that work anything like in the movies and comics?

I hoped they had better tactics in real life. I suspected Kirby did, though I wasn't sure why I suspected that.

"Kirby hasn't been doing this for long," Scarlett said. "She has to recognize the pull, screen the person she's drawn to, convince them, train them…"

And if she was the only one doing the recruiting, that would be time-consuming. Training sounded kind of fun. Learning to use magic… "Have you been training?"

"Yes. I think Kirby's grateful Arnlaug can do a lot of it. And Pan. They're both so talented."

Seeing the dreamy look in Scarlett's eyes when she talked about her guys left a whisper of longing in me. Not just for the romance, but also for the closeness she had with them. Like that, I felt like I was on the outside looking in again.

"You're going to love everyone." Scarlett snagged another bite of my food.

I wasn't going to be the downer today. This would be fun. "I'm looking forward to all of it."

We chatted more about random things—books and comics and Scarlett's next book tour—and finished breakfast. Then we headed downstairs, to the hotel's dining room. As we pushed inside, the chatter stopped, and all eyes were on us.

Awkward.

"This is Mia." Scarlett gestured to me without missing a beat. "Mia, this is everyone."

I recognized Kirby. And Scarlett. There was no way I was going to remember all their names.

A shorter, curvy woman with vibrant red hair, a scar running across her face, and a nose ring broke from the group and joined us. She pulled me into a tight hug. "I'm Astrid. So happy to meet you," she said at a normal volume. She leaned closer. "Whatever your reasons were for turning down Kirby, they're your own." That comment was only meant for my ears.

"Does everyone here know about that?" Embarrassment crept up inside.

Astrid shook her head. "No one else besides Scarlett, Kirby, Brit, and me."

That was almost half the room.

"And only because Brit and I helped find you when Kirby felt you the first time. I promise, to all of us, you're a friend." She pulled away and pointed both of us toward the room.

She introduced everyone—Elin, Magnus, Brigid, Tatiana, Maeve, Azzie—and I barely remembered anyone. Brit stood out—the petite curvy girl with blond hair who was *not super magic, but she's as immortal as it gets and can pick an apple off your head at three hundred meters with an AK-47.*

What an introduction. "That sounds terrifying," I said.

"To be fair, I'm only using an AK if I have to. And I don't miss." Brit grinned. "You'd be surprised how often it's necessary to bring a gun to a god fight."

Astrid made a snort-laugh sound. "I doubt that reassures Mia." She picked out the one person she hadn't introduced yet. A goth woman in the kind of tulle skirt and fishnet tights I wished I had the nerve to wear. "And that's Dahlia. She's a dragon."

No shit. "Dragons are real." I tried to hide my awe but failed.

Dahlia grinned. "If you think that's epic, you're about to be blown away by awesome."

"You being here is perfect timing." Astrid tugged me further into the room, to join the group. Everyone shook my hand. Offered hugs. They all seemed genuinely happy to meet boring, human me.

They were about to be blown away by the boring. "Perfect timing for what?"

"We're trying to decide what to do. You're the tie-breaking vote." I was pretty sure that was Elin speaking.

"What are my options? I don't vote for the shooting an apple off my head thing. Ever."

"Wise." Kirby's voice came from behind, startling me. "You get juice in your hair. Pulp. It's kind of gross."

"Apple pulp, I assume." I hoped. "Why do you sound like you're speaking from experience?"

Someone else let out a short laugh. She had auburn hair, and two tattoos peeked above the collar of her T-shirt. One looked like the swan-like head of a bird, but it was red and orange and yellow like flame, and on the other side of her neck, I saw a more abstract pattern in vibrant purples, blues, and greens.

Astrid shot her a stern look, and the woman shrugged. There were at least three redheads in here besides Astrid, and I'd already mixed up which was which.

"We can play D&D—the biggest game the hotel has ever seen—and that's the first and only choice," Dahlia said.

"Or we can paint each other's nails," Elin offered.

Both were much better choices than playing William Tell with modern firearms, whether or not the person on the other end of the gun was a skilled marksman. I couldn't imagine that a Valkyrie would keep nice nails if they were fighting, but I also wasn't a nice-nail person. Scarlett managed to keep hers immaculate.

Which also meant, as much as I loved the first

option, she was probably leaning toward the second. "Why don't half of you do one, and the other half do the other, and then everyone gets what they want?" I asked.

"I told you she was the smart one." Scarlett beamed.

"Which group are you going with, Mia?" Astrid asked.

If she'd helped do the research on me, she probably already knew. I felt bad splitting off from Scarlett though.

Scarlett nudged me toward Astrid. "We'll catch up more when we're done, I promise," Scarlett said. "Dahlia will show you where you can play."

The group of us that broke off for D&D consisted of Dahlia, Brit, Astrid, Tatiana, me, and… Magnus, that was her name. The redhead with the wicked looking claw ring on one index finger and the vibrant tattoos near her neck.

"I can't believe you're really a dragon," I said to Dahlia as we left the main building and headed outside. "Do you breathe fire? Do you have a hoard?" Most people might think those were ridiculous questions, but if Valkyries and gods existed, why wouldn't dragons?

"Kind of?" Dahlia twisted her mouth. "I summon fire. I hoard data like you wouldn't believe."

"Mostly, she changes her hair color on a whim and takes her clothes off in public," Brit teased.

Magnus and Astrid laughed.

Tatiana shrugged. "Don't ask me. I'm here for the weirdo club, but I haven't figured out yet if this one is cool-ranch or spicy-nacho flavored."

"I guarantee you, we're not *cool* anything." Dahlia steered us down a side path. "And I don't do it in public. And I don't take off *all* my clothes. And it's not like it's some random crazy person thing. My boyfriends own a burlesque club. I dance there."

"Boyfriends." I didn't mean to say that out loud. She had more than one—like Scarlett did.

Tatiana sighed. "Several of them have multiple guys. Lucky bitches."

"Not all luck is good." Brit's retort sounded light-hearted.

Astrid stepped sideways, to nudge her. "Brit thinks boys are icky."

"Brit only has eyes for Kirby," Magnus added.

"You're going to overwhelm the new girl, and then she'll think we're all nuts." Dahlia stopped in front of a door marked *Reading Room,* that led to a new building set a little away from the others.

Magnus pushed the door open. "We are all nuts. But the good kind. Cashews or macadamias or something."

"As opposed to the kind that gets hairs stuck in the back of your throat," Brit said.

Tatiana made a gagging noise. "Thanks for the visual."

"You're welcome." Brit grinned.

We stepped into the room. It was the perfect place for a group of people to sit however they considered comfortable, on a variety of brightly colored chairs and floor pillows, and relax and read.

Or, in our case, game.

It wasn't quite as cool as meeting an actual dragon, but it was close. I needed a place like this for my comic shop.

We were missing a few key things for a TTRPG, though. "Is this more of a freeform roleplay?" Because I could see that falling apart fast with this group. Not that I'd mind. "Are there dice stashed somewhere?"

"Check this out." Dahlia grinned. She reached into the bag hanging from her shoulder, and kept reaching, until most of her arm vanished in a purse not nearly big enough for that to happen. She rummaged around, then pulled out a box of dice. Followed by a pouch of more dice, a notepad, a rulebook… And she kept going until an entire setup was on the coffee table in front of her.

"You have an actual bag of holding? No shit." I was going to have to make an entirely new list of coolest things I'd ever seen. Which made me wonder… "Why do you play something like D&D if you're living the reality?"

Astrid laughed. "Don't call me out like that."

"Besides, we've modified the rules a teensy bit," Magnus said.

"Dahlia pouts if we fight dragons." Astrid grabbed dice and picked out a large pillow to sit on.

Dahlia huffed and flopped onto a nearby beanbag. "I just don't understand why you pick on the dragons. It's not our fault we're awesome."

"Besides, D&D dragons are way tougher than Dahlia," Brit teased.

"Hey." Dahlia pouted. Horns sprouted from her head, and wings from her back. A tail appeared, curling around her leg. She was half-dragon, half-human.

Another amazing thing for the list. "They're kind of right. That's more cute than terrifying."

"But she gets the award for Most Adorable." Astrid reached across the table to pinch one of Dahlia's lightly-scaled cheeks. "Baby dragon want a cookie?"

Dahlia huffed and pulled away with crossed arms. "Seriously? Also, yes. Of course I want a cookie."

There was so much teasing in here, but none of it was cruel. I liked the way these women got along like it was natural.

I wanted to be a part of it. "We can go on a quest to find cookies for the dragon?"

Dahlia clapped. "She wins. She's our new DM."

"Cookie heist?" Astrid sat up straight.

Brit found a spot as well. "Best kind of heist ever. I'm in."

"Rivaled only by chocolate-chip muffins." Tatiana

situated herself near Brit. "And y'all are definitely spicy nacho."

Everyone seemed to already have characters they were willing to play in a one-off, and within a few minutes I had sheets for each of them in my email. It was convenient, and a slight relief. If we had to roll stats and make up backstories, that could take a group like this another two days.

Though it'd probably be a lot of fun.

I wasn't the writer Scarlett was, but I could tell a story when the need arose. "All right, intrepid adventurers, your quest sounds far simpler than it actually is. Your loyal dragon companion needs cookies."

"To save my life." Dahlia raised her hand. "I will literally die without cookies."

Ridiculous. I loved it. "But the only cookies in the land are kept in The Baker's Vault. Are you all ready to take that risk?"

"I've got my *sweetest* spells ready," Astrid said.

Tatiana scrunched up her nose. "I'm fresh out of puns, but I have a bow."

"Can I just shoot something?" Brit asked.

Magnus vanished from the room.

What the—?

No one else looked fazed. Should I say something? "Where did she go?"

"Wait for it." Dahlia puffed out her cheeks with a sigh.

Seconds later, Magnus reappeared with a plate of the cookies. I had no idea where she'd gotten them, but they still had steam rising from them and smelled heavenly. She handed one to Dahlia. "Mission accomplished. I'm not letting a cookie craving kill my sister."

A round of groans circled the room, but Dahlia didn't hesitate to shove half of a giant cookie in her mouth in one bite.

She coughed up crumbs when a flying pillow hit her in the face. "Hey." Her protest was muffled.

Another pillow flew at Magnus, who vanished before it hit her. She reappeared across the room, set the plate down, grabbed a pillow, and blinked out of sight again.

"Crap. They're hunting us." Astrid crawled toward me and stacked pillows around us. "Quick. We need a fort."

"What good does a fort do when they can teleport?" I was missing something.

"None at all." Dahlia's voice came from behind, and a giant cushion fell on our heads.

The room erupted in giggles, squeals, and pillows, and I found myself laughing along with everyone else, in the middle of the biggest, most ridiculous pillow fight ever.

When everything finally died down, we all lay on the floor, laughing and gasping for breath.

"Who would've guessed the Ragnarök the

Valkyries would bring about would be so… soft?" Astrid tossed a pillow in the air and caught it.

"Ragnarök is about rebirth. But we're not soft. Just compassionate and human," Tatiana said. "Every single one of us will still do what we need to when the time comes."

Astrid threw a projectile at her. "I meant the pillow fight, but I do like your poetic interpretation of the end of the world."

"Defeating evil, one pillow slap at a time." Magnus had the plate of cookies again. "You know, the magical-girl way."

This was insane and random and so incredible. Magical was the perfect word for it, in a way I'd never thought of magic before.

We spent the next few hours trying to play but alternating between joking and answering questions. I had so many, but this world was new to Tatiana, too. The others had been raised human, but Brit, Magnus, and Dahlia had been brought up by the gods. To kill people like us.

They'd gotten out, but most magic wasn't news to them. And Astrid… She'd lived multiple lives. Been alive back when Vikings existed. Had originally grown up in a world where magic was everyday. And she was a witch.

How cool would that be?

Apparently, Valkyries weren't the only thing growing in numbers; more dragons were appearing too. Azzie was dating one, and so was Astrid. Dahlia's aunts were dragons older than humanity. The claw ring Magnus wore gave her dragon-like powers, because it was made of Dahlia's claw.

And the stories they told about the gods... It seemed like a very love-hate relationship all of these women had with the deities they'd encountered. As in, most of them had fallen for and loved at least one god, and they hated most of the others.

"Scarlett told me she fought Odin, that he was dead, but she never went into details." I didn't blame her. Being yanked into a new reality and having to face off against a being that powerful all at once would traumatize most people.

This time Astrid's scoff was soft and flat. "Odin's not dead."

ELEVEN
MIA

"What did you say?" Kirby stood in the doorway.

The mood in the room fell flat, as if a switch had been flipped.

"The war, the blood sacrifice, didn't kill him, all those centuries ago," Astrid said. "Why does anyone think a sword would—magic or otherwise? I don't care if a mountain fell on him. Until I see the body, he's alive. Besides, I can't find his ravens. Muninn especially with the strong bond we shared, that he showed was still there when I found him over the summer, before the shit that went down with Odin. You can't convince me that intelligent birds like them don't still have the familiar bond intact." She clenched her hands into tight fists. "After everything Odin did to me, I can't ignore this feeling."

"She's got a point." Magnus straightened up and

brushed crumbs from the front of her shirt. "Corpse or it didn't happen."

"What's so bad about Odin?" My blood ran cold when so many shocked expressions stared back at me. "Not that I'm saying he isn't bad. From what little Scarlett told me…" Fuck.

Kirby leaned against the door frame with a sigh. "Let's start with the fact that the one-eyed fucker cursed me because I had the audacity to be my own person. Over time, he destroyed every single one of my sisters who dared to defy him. He killed Astrid as a child each time she was reborn, he used mind control on Arnlaug to get him to kidnap Scarlett… That's only the tip of the iceberg."

Arnlaug kidnapped Scarlett? Wait. One-eyed… Ravens… "What does he look like?" Memories from the other night tickled my thoughts.

"Old. Bitter. But he has ways of hiding his appearance. Looking like someone else. Not his own magic, but he's always happy to steal it from someone," Astrid said. "The one thing he can't hide is the missing eye."

"And the ravens." I was talking to myself as much as them. "I think he came into my shop the other day."

"When?" Kirby's voice was hard.

An eternity ago.

Only a few days ago.

"The night before you showed up." Oh. That was bad, wasn't it? I had no idea what it meant, but it didn't seem good.

Kirby pushed away from the wall and took a few steps into the room before stopping with a frown. "Mia, can I talk to you for a few minutes? Someplace else?"

"Yeah. Of course." I followed her into a new, smaller room. This looked more like it was for staging or storage, with several rows of stacked up chairs filling most of the small space.

"I need you to tell me everything about the man you met." There was no room for argument in Kirby's tone.

"There's not much to tell. He gave off a weird vibe that made me not want to talk to him alone. He insisted he wanted a present for his niece. He would say one thing then do a total one-eighty and say the opposite…" Pulling up the memory brought more vivid sensations with it than I expected, and nausea gnawed at my gut. "For a few seconds, I almost felt like he was trying to climb into my head."

"The things he said—like what?"

It should be a little fuzzy, but it was all still real and solid. "Like when I told him I was closing, he said I wasn't. He said it with so much confidence, like he thought he was a Jedi or an asshole romance hero or something. When I disagreed with him, he changed his tune in a blink and apologized."

"Odin can use mind control," Kirby said.

Oh. Oh. Fuck. The implications of that sank in, and I leaned against the nearest wall for support. "I don't think he… Would I remember?" Was that why the night was so vivid? The memory wasn't real? I was going to be sick.

"You would remember." Kirby's response was only mildly comforting. "Maybe that's not what he was doing to you. But you wanted to know what makes Odin so bad? That's just one thing. When he created Valkyries, he made us to serve him. He couldn't mind control us all—as far as I know that's more of a one-at-a-time thing, and it has limits. But we belonged to him. We weren't allowed to love anyone else or be with anyone else or serve anyone else—even ourselves. We were Odin's."

"That sounds horrible."

She shrugged. "It wasn't great, no."

"So wait… How long ago was that? How old are you?"

Kirby's laugh was strained. "That was more than a thousand years ago. Currently, in this body? I'm thirty. This is the first life where I've lived this long since my original one."

I could ask so many questions, but I had a feeling I wouldn't pick the right one if I got too detailed. "What happened?"

"Starkad and I fell in love. Back then," she said. "I don't know what you see when you look at him, but I see a man who would move heaven and earth and anyone who got in his way, for me. I'd do the same for him. I *did* do the same for him. He died on the battlefield, and instead of taking him to Valhalla, like I was supposed to, I gave him immortality."

Holy shit, that was power. But more than that, it was love. I couldn't imagine someone doing that for me, though the thought of feeling that way about another being was both implausible and made me ache for it in a way I never thought possible. "Wow."

"Yeah. So Odin cursed me, to help me *learn my lesson*." Bitterness filled Kirby's voice. "The curse was that I'd be reborn again and again until I learned what it was to be a Valkyrie. He should've been more specific, though I'm glad he wasn't. I think he really meant until I learned to serve him and be a loyal little puppet. Instead, in this life, I finally figured it out."

This was deep. And it made it easy to see why she didn't like Odin. The hurt in her voice said there was so much more to the story, and the look in her eyes, that kind of distant stare that saw something that wasn't in this room, spoke volumes.

"What does it mean to be a Valkyrie?" I'd passed on the opportunity. It wasn't as though her answer made a difference at this point, but I needed to know.

She jammed her hands in her pockets. "It's different for every single one of us, so my answer might not match Astrid's or Elin's or Brigid's. But every one of them out there, and me… We all want to keep people who don't deserve it from being hurt."

"It's a nice dream." Like in the comics. I didn't see how it was real, but I wanted it to be, so badly.

Kirby nodded. "It's a real thing."

From what I'd seen today, I believed that they believed it. I wanted to as well, especially after spending the afternoon with some of them. For those few hours, I was a part of something bigger, and not just because we were having fun. There was a thread that connected me to them. A bond.

I might be imagining it, but talking to Kirby now, I could almost pretend it was real. She'd managed to gather all of them together, so there had to be something there.

"The place we grew up in this life…" Kirby drew in a long breath through her nostrils. "Me, Brit, Magnus, and Dahlia… That place was made to break us. Not just the four of us, but everyone there. It was a place made to tear down every single student, destroy our sense of self, and take what was left to use us to serve the gods who put us there."

The parallel was impossible to miss. "Kind of like Odin in your first life."

"A lot like that, yeah." Kirby's smile was dry. "I thought I could save Brit from it. I thought I could shield her and protect her and that none of the shit would ever land on her."

Why did I suspect the rest of this story wasn't as sweet as that sounded?

"I was so busy protecting her from one shitstorm that I missed a worse one. And she didn't need me to shield her," Kirby said. "She needed me to stand next to her and trust that she was strong enough to be by my side." Kirby shook her head. "Not sure that metaphor is working."

"I think I get it."

Kirby let out another sigh. "I keep making decisions like that for people. Most of the time the consequences aren't as drastic as they were with Brit, but I'm used to taking the lead. The person in charge has to pick directions and can't waver.... But I also need to learn I'm not an island. There's something I don't like about that, though. If I thought I could fight Odin alone, I would. If I thought I could take on the other gods, those who would rather be kings of the ashes than admit they're not all-powerful, I'd take them all on alone. Because I hate the idea that any of you, that anyone, might get hurt because I'm not strong enough."

Something told me this was a side of Kirby she didn't show to many people, including herself. I heard the hurt in her voice, and the frustration, but I also heard the passion. I got it. For so long I wanted to be someone who could help. Who could keep other people from getting hurt.

I still wanted that, but I'd given up on thinking I could have it.

"We're not made to face this world alone, though." The way Kirby looked at me, a combination of softness and determination shone in her eyes. "Especially when it comes to taking on the gods."

There was no metaphor there. But, "I've always been alone." I snapped my jaw shut. That was a feeling meant for me and no one else.

"I'm sorry." Kirby sounded sincere. "I'm sorry you've had to be that, but you aren't alone now. Regardless of if you're a Valkyrie or not, you still have us. This instinct that drives me to find all of you, this gift that lets me share my power with you, thinks you should be one of us, and I believe it. Nothing I've seen from you, nothing I know about you, makes me think that seeking you out was a mistake. You're strong enough, you're capable enough, and most importantly, you're human enough.

"The decision to do this is still yours—I'm not trying to take that from you. Now that you've had time to think about it, to better understand who we are, I'm going to ask you again. If you tell me *no* again, I respect that. Will you let me make you a Valkyrie?"

"Yes." The answer came easily. It was what I should've told her the first time, and I knew it. I'd let self-doubt win. The feeling I'd fought for my entire life that said I wasn't enough. But this was something I'd always wanted, and this group of people made me believe I could find it here—the means to help the world be a better place. "Yes. I'd like to be a Valkyrie."

"Give me your hand." Kirby held out her own.

I hovered my palm centimeters above hers. "Will this hurt?"

"It hasn't yet, but every one of these is different. So I'll just say probably not."

That wasn't reassuring, but I appreciated her honesty. I placed my hand in hers.

A shock jolted through me, and sparks filled the air where we made contact. I yelped and pulled away out of instinct.

Was that a scorch mark on my skin? The smell of ozone filled the air. "Sorry. I didn't expect…"

Kirby frowned. "That's not…" She grasped my offered hand again.

The results were the same, but this time I held on. For one second, then three, then five, as the shock grew stronger and more painful.

Kirby let go and took a few steps back. "It's not…" She bit her bottom lip.

"It's not working." Whispers of disappointment and *told you so* gnawed at my thoughts. "Do I need to take off my jewelry? Maybe it's the synthetic clothing?" I was grasping. More desperate than I wanted to be.

"I've had this reaction to me before." Kirby didn't

close the distance between us again. "Before I understood what I could do, before we knew Dahlia was a dragon, I tried to do this with her, and this same thing happened. With Zeke—Azzie's boyfriend. When I try to heal Brit… In their cases, my magic is incompatible with theirs."

"I'm not a dragon."

"They didn't know yet," Kirby said.

Good for them. "I'm not anything. I'm not a dragon, I'm not magic. I'm a big awkward girl from nowhere."

Kirby shook her head. "Don't go anywhere."

I was in a storage closet in a hotel in Greece. Home was thousands of miles away, and magic brought me here. Where was I going to go? "All right."

Kirby left, and returned a moment later with Astrid.

"I want to see if you've got some of the other immortal traits, like instant healing." Kirby grasped my hand again. This time there were no sparks. "May I?"

"I broke my arm when I was ten. I had stitches in my leg when I was fifteen. I currently have at least three paper cuts from doing inventory last week." I pulled up my sleeve to expose the old scratches.

Kirby brushed her fingers over the skin, and there were more sparks. Those hurt a lot, and I sucked in a sharp breath at the pain, trying to suppress a stronger reaction.

"Here." Astrid touched the spots, and glowing golden threads seemed to radiate from her hands to wrap around and vanish into my arms. The ache was gone and so were the wounds.

Did that mean… "Is that a good sign?"

"It means my witch powers work on you," Astrid said.

Kirby was still staring at my healed arm. "I don't understand," she muttered. "You're supposed to be…"

But I understood. Realization sank in and rested in my stomach like a heavy stone. "I told you I'm not Valkyrie material." It hurt more than I thought possible to say those worse.

"You are. I haven't been wrong about this."

"We're all wrong sometimes. I think I should go home." Because if I stayed here, surrounded by these glorious beings, the fact that I wasn't good enough would gnaw at me. At least, if I left now, I could start getting over the ache of disappointment. I could give in to the voice that asked, *Why would you think you could be one of them*? And I could do so in private, rather than breaking down here.

I refused to talk to anyone, while I gathered my things from my room. When Dahlia dropped me off in front of my house, I couldn't return her hug. I didn't want her pity.

And when I stepped inside, and found Thac and

Caleb sifting through my house, their lies from the last time I saw them rushed back.

"What are you doing?" I didn't have the restraint left to approach this with any sort of rationale, but I refused to let them see how much this disappointment was breaking me.

TWELVE
THAC

TWELVE HOURS.

That was how long I'd been looking for Mia since my conversation with Ronan.

She wasn't answering her phone. None of the friends I'd called knew where she was. I'd even called Scarlett, though I knew Mia wasn't in Greece. How could she be? But Scarlett's hotel said she was unavailable.

Caleb had fallen asleep again while I was gone, and I wasn't surprised. He needed to sleep off the magic I'd used on him. I wanted to find out why he looked like a dragon, but tracking down Mia was more important. If Kirby had already gotten to her… If Odin had…

Ronan tended to be an idealist, and at times he fell in with those people who convinced him they were too. Odin may be a reformed god, but I'd believe it when I saw it, and not at any point before then.

I paced the living room, racking my brain for ideas of where to look for Mia next. If something happened to her, I'd destroy whoever—whatever—hurt her.

Footsteps that were out of sync with mine scuffed on the carpet, and Caleb appeared in the bedroom doorway. He'd pulled his shirt back on, but hadn't done up the buttons. It would make him tempting in so many other circumstances, but today I had another focus.

"How'd your meeting go?" His voice was tired, and he looked nothing like the man I'd taken out of Mia's comic shop just a day ago.

"It was disconcerting. If Mia were to go on vacation, where would she go?"

"Throw yourself at a guy almost drunk, and he's still focused on your roommate," Caleb muttered. He focused on me, "Why? Is this a game?"

"She's missing."

Caleb scrubbed his face, then began doing up his shirt. "*Vacation* is not *missing*. If she didn't tell you where she went, maybe there's a reason."

I wanted to throttle him for his casual attitude. "She is in danger, not because I'm overbearing and possessive, but because someone is looking for her. Someone dangerous."

"Who?"

"I can't say."

"Does she know?" Now concern was filtering into Caleb's voice.

"No."

He raised his brows. "Does it have to do with her father?"

"Not the way you think. There's no time for this." I wouldn't play the same back and forth question games with him that he'd forced when I asked who he was. I needed answers *now*. "Do you know where she'd go on vacation?"

"She has a list of places she loves, and I can't tell you which she would pick." Caleb frowned. "Wait. Mia doesn't do vacations. I've *never* seen her take a day off."

That was my bigger concern. The one I hadn't dared voice. She wasn't the kind of person who would pick up in the middle of the week and just vanish unless something extreme happened. "We need to find her."

"Have you checked the house?" Caleb grabbed his sweater vest and draped it over his arm. "We can see if she's left any hints there. Or if there's any indication that…"

Why hadn't I already looked in her place? I waited half a second for him to finish the thought. "That what?"

"That she's been taken."

I didn't want to hear those words spoken aloud, but he'd vocalized my fear and it was more possible than he realized. "Let's go."

This would let me keep an eye on him, and when Mia was safe, I could resume pushing this man to figure out what he was. I didn't think he was lying to me about not knowing, and whatever lock keeping him restrained seemed solidly secured. But it was obviously cracking and there was no telling if it would break in a year or an hour.

I took Caleb to the fae doorway and back to Mia's street.

"So… hang on," he said as we walked toward the shop and their home. "Is this how you randomly show up? Why she swears sometimes you're watching, even though you're supposed to be halfway across the country?"

She'd noticed my presence even when I didn't visit? I liked the idea more than I should admit.

"Yes," I said.

His *hmm* didn't tell me what he was thinking, though his previous comments gave me an idea. I didn't care if he thought I was over the top—I would do anything to keep Mia safe and the longer she was gone, the more defined that list of *anything* became.

A moment later, we were in her house, looking while trying not to disturb, for any sign of where she might have gone.

There was no indication of anything, except that the place felt disturbingly lacking in her presence.

"What are you both doing in here?" Mia's voice came from behind us.

I spun to see her standing in her doorway, suitcase on the ground next to her, and she was staring at us with a furrowed brow. "Did you let him in, Caleb? What the hell is up with you two?"

She didn't look or sound hurt.

"You vanished. We were worried," Caleb said.

Mia stepped inside with a sigh. "I sent you a text. I'm fine. Disappointed, but fine." She closed the door behind her and set her suitcase aside.

Caleb patted his pockets. "Fuck. I must've left my phone…" He looked at me and trailed off.

"You didn't send me a text," I said.

"Because I don't check in with you every time I go somewhere." Mia sounded more tired than annoyed.

Behind her, Caleb smirked.

Irritating man.

"Where were you?" I felt no remorse at being worried about her.

"I wasn't here. Look, I'm tired, and if you two aren't going to tell me things like why you've spent more time together in the last day then the entire rest of the time I've known Caleb, I'm going to take a nap."

I was relieved that she didn't seem harmed, but I wasn't leaving her alone. "Not here." Just because she'd avoided the threat so far didn't mean she would continue to do so.

"No, really. Tell me what's going on, or go away." Mia raked her fingers through her hair.

There were some things I couldn't tell her, those things I'd promised Ronan were between us, but perhaps it was time for her to know some truths. "I will tell you. I give you my word, if you will please come with us."

"Come on." Caleb's voice was light and playful. "*Come with me if you vant to live*. How are you going to turn down a line that classic?"

One corner of Mia's mouth pulled up. "Answers better include why the two of you are chummy."

"We are most certainly not *chummy*." The thought bothered me.

"We promise answers, though," Caleb said.

Mia dragged in a deep breath. "Fine. Let me check on the shop, and then I'll go with you. Where are we going?"

"Back to my place, through a fae door." I braced myself for an argument similar to the one I'd had with Caleb about magic.

She glanced at me, lips pursed.

Why did she look irritated rather than surprised? Perhaps she thought I was making things up, and was about to argue that I'd promised the truth and didn't seem to be offering it.

Mia gave a brief shake of her head, and walked

out the front door. Caleb locked everything up, and the three of us walked the short path to her comic store.

The interior of the other building smelled like stale smoke and fresh chemicals. There was no sign there had been a fire or any damage behind the register.

Mia did a quick survey of the entire building, then turned to us. "Truth time. Start with why you lit my place on fire."

"It was an accident. I was stressed out," Caleb said.

Most certainly the truth. I wished it came with more answers.

Mia looked skeptical. "So you started a fire?"

"Apparently? Not consciously. It just kind of came out of my hands."

I didn't imagine that Mia would take that kind of explanation well. She twisted her mouth, and I prepared again for the argument and disbelief. "You're right, Thac, we should go back to your place and talk about this."

"You believe him?" I didn't understand what was going on. Why was I the one who seemed surprised by *her* actions? "You're not going to demand an explanation or insist that people don't spontaneously cast flames?"

"He promised the truth, and Caleb doesn't strike me as the kind of guy who keeps important secrets." Mia's answer was anything but satisfactory.

A knock on the front door interrupted the conversation. A man who radiated an air of far-older-than-he-looked peered through the glass.

"God damn it," Mia muttered. "He's the asshole who came by the other night. I think he's—" She snapped her jaw shut with the shake of her head.

"You think he's what?" I was the one holding the answers, but I also felt like I was the one in the dark.

"I'm going to tell him to fuck off." Mia turned toward the door.

I grabbed her arm. Whoever he was, if he'd harassed her before, that was bad enough. But the fact that he radiated deception meant I wanted her as far from him as possible. "Let me get rid of him."

Mia stared at me, jaw clenched. "Okay."

I didn't expect zero argument. Where had she been and what happened there?

As I drew closer to the door, the appearance of the man shifted. It wasn't anything drastic, more like a blurred image coming into focus. When I had a sharper view of him, the one eye plus the raven sitting on his shoulder pinged in my mind with a single name: *Odin*.

I opened the door, and he studied me. "Who are you?" he asked.

"Tlaloc." If this was Odin, and I had no reason to believe otherwise, we both looked different than the last time we'd met, hundreds of years ago. I wasn't surprised he didn't recognize me. My name didn't carry the same recognition his did. "This property and its owner are under my protection. You need to leave." The phrasing would sound odd to a random stranger, but to another god there was warning in my words.

He gave a brief nod. "I see. I'm Odin, and I'm only here to protect the woman."

"*The woman* has a name," Mia called from behind me. "As you can see, I have plenty of protection. You're not welcome here. Don't come back."

I wasn't surprised she hadn't completely let me handle things. Her fire was as alluring as the rest of her.

"Your guardians aren't who you think they are." Odin looked past me to Mia. "Especially not that one." He nodded at Caleb, and muttered a series of words I couldn't make out.

A horrifying roar tore from Caleb's throat, clashing and mingling with the caw of the ravens. The birds tore into the shop, circled Mia, and flew out again. They and Odin vanished as they reached the door.

I wanted to chase, but a glance at Caleb said I needed to stay here for Mia's sake. He was shifting into the same form I saw earlier—a humanoid dragon.

"Oh, fuck me." Mia's voice was more awe than fear. "You're a dragon."

How the fuck was that her response?

Caleb's reply sounded like words, but not a language I knew. He fell to his knees and dug his fingers into the carpet. Claws extended, indenting and then cutting. A disconcerting cracking whispered in the air.

Mia took a step toward him, and I grabbed her again. She jerked away from me and knelt in front of Caleb. "How long have you been able to do this?" Her voice was calm and kind. Too much so for someone who was learning about magic while the man who rented a room from her turned into a monster.

Unless she already knew…

She pressed her palm to his cheek, and his claws receded. His horns vanished back into his head.

"I don't know what it is." Caleb's reply was a dry rasp.

Mia stroked a thumb over his cheek. "We need to figure it out." She was right. But not here.

"We're leaving now. Lock everything. We'll talk where it's safe." I wasn't hearing any arguments this time. I had to get her out of here, and if that meant bringing him, so be it.

I threw my coat over him, to hide the new extremities as much as possible. Few people would take notice of us unless we impacted their day directly, but it only took one observant person with their phone at the ready, and in a few hours, the area around Mia's shop would become a hotspot for people looking for more clues about what happened.

Not safe for her at all.

Was there a little part of me also worried about Caleb? Yes, though I wouldn't admit it aloud if asked.

The three of us hurried toward the fae door in the alley, and stepped through.

As we emerged in my apartment, Mia looked around, curiosity etched on her face. "I always wondered where this went."

This was not how I imagined this conversation going. I gave Mia my full attention. "Where were you, and why are you unsurprised by any of this?" I wasn't playing games this time, I wanted answers.

"You first." She studied me with that strong defiance that made her even sexier. "Who are you?"

"I am a *god*." I expected the same response Caleb had given me. Or at least a touch of awe.

Instead, Mia continued to look me over, her expression barely shifting. "Hmm. Of what?"

"Of harvest. Of prosperity. Of the storms."

"Cool. And Caleb is a dragon?"

I did not understand the direction of this conversation. "No. He may be something similar, but there are only three dragons."

Mia gave her attention to Caleb, who had returned to a human form and was sitting on the couch, head in his hands. She knelt in front of him. "How are you doing?"

"Far more confused than you seem to be." He cracked a smile.

He had a point. This was *nothing* like the conversation I pictured having with Mia about magic.

THIRTEEN
CALEB

THERE WAS THAT WORD AGAIN. *DRAGON.*

A much younger me was screaming in excitement. Pre-pubescent me was scoffing—*there can't be dragons and God.* And all adult me could think was *sure, that might as well be a thing at this point.*

And on top of it all, I wanted to know why Mia was taking this news so much better than I had. I was still struggling with the truth of it all, and she looked like someone just told her the sun rose every morning. As in *Yeah, seen it. And?*

"First of all, I'm pretty sure there are more than three dragons." Mia's response didn't explain anything. "Because I know of at least three."

"What? How?" Was this some sort of internet prank?

As the ridiculousness set in, a fresh wave of fury surged back. It was potent and not like current me at all. The voice wanted to burn it all down. It was like the guy at the door—was he really Odin?—had triggered something inside me.

Fortunately, I'd spent years learning to control the cloying rage that haunted me when I was younger. I focused on yanking threads of fury until they evaporated, and I could think more clearly. "I think you need to answer Thac's questions, Mia. Where were you and why doesn't any of this surprise you?"

She raised her brows. Yeah, I was agreeing with the big sexy bruiser.

"Tell me you're all right, first." The way she watched me with dark, soulful eyes, softened my swelling fury.

"I'll be better when I have answers. Not just from you, but about me." I dragged in another calming breath. "Until then, I'm stable. That's a good thing, right?"

One corner of her mouth pulled up, but the amusement didn't reach her eyes. "It doesn't sound like a bad thing." She stood and looked between us—me fighting curling up like a useless lump, and Thac standing with his arms crossed, looking like a statue. An effigy built to himself.

"I guess I can tell?" Mia twisted her mouth. "No one is treating any of what I've learned recently like a secret, though it seems like the kind of thing that should be. A few weeks ago, Scarlett became a Valkyrie."

Thac tensed—impressive trick for a stone statue.

Mia was pacing and had her back to him.

"She what?" His voice was rock as well.

"A Valkyrie." Mia repeated. "Warrior who ferries the dead to Valhalla and apparently other things as well."

Dragons were real. Mythological gods were real. A one-eyed man with ravens made me lose my humanity… Wait. Valkyries. Odin?

I was losing my mind.

"How did that happen?" Thac's tone matched the chaos in my head. Did stress give gods heart attacks?

Pausing in her pacing, Mia tapped her fingers on her leg. She furrowed her brow. "This probably goes without saying, but I don't know how much of this I should say. You both promise not to tell anyone?"

"I'm going to run up to every person on the street, shake them, and say *Your world is a lie—gods walk among us*." I couldn't stop the sarcasm from bleeding into my voice. "Because I want to be locked up."

Huh. Maybe that was why they—whoever *they* were—didn't care who Mia told.

She resumed her pacing. "There's this other Valkyrie, and she's one of the originals from way back when. As in, Odin created her more than a thousand years ago. She died. She came back. And she has the ability to make other Valkyries."

"You're taking this really well." I was a little jealous of how collected Mia seemed about this whole thing. Did meeting Valkyries come with a dose of Valium? It was a funny thing to think, but I almost fell into an insane laughter at the thought.

"I've had weeks to get used to the idea, and really, it feels like it's always been real. It felt more right to hear the information than to think otherwise." Mia paused again and looked at me. I could almost hear her daring me to disagree. To call her crazy. To say this was all in our heads.

The best I could offer was, "But… magic."

"Right?" Her grin was as bright as if someone had flipped a switch. "Isn't it incredible?"

"I struggle to believe no one cared that Scarlett told you this." Thac's tone was impossible to read.

Mia fixed him with a long look. "I struggle to believe you never have. Not a single mention and then today *I'm a god*. Like… what the fuck? Besides, it's kind of like one of those unintentional secrets. If they tell people, and someone believes, they get to be in on the secret. Most people, they're not going to believe. And do I interpret correctly that you told Caleb? But not me?"

If I was still training to be a priest, I'd find a metaphor for faith in there, but this wasn't a metaphor, it was a literal. "He told me because I'm living it, and I still struggle with it being real."

"How are you struggling with it?" Mia's question was kind rather than accusing. "You grew a fucking tail."

She had a good point, and I didn't have a comeback.

"Besides, we're not to the truly unbelievable part yet," Mia said. "Then Kirby offered to make me into a Valkyrie too."

"No." Thac sounded abruptly horrified.

Weird time to have a reaction like that. "Are you a superhero now?" Apparently I could wrap my head around that. In the short time I'd known Mia, that was one thing that rang out truer about her than anything else—she would save the world if she could.

Mia's snort was laced with something dark and resentful. "Me? No. It didn't stick."

"Good," Thac said.

She whirled on him with a scowl. "Do you have a problem with Valkyries? Did one friend zone you a century ago or something?"

Thac clenched his jaw.

Stoic and frustratingly sexy. I didn't miss Mia's frustration either. The three of us would have incredible grudge sex.

I should feel bad for thinking that, but apparently whatever was happening to me had broken my moral compass.

"So much for you telling me the truth." Mia huffed.

"What do you mean it didn't stick?" I wanted more story. More details. Maybe if I got enough of them, this would feel real, rather than like a long, weird dream.

That was the problem though—it did feel real. Half of me knew this was actually the world, and my entire life experience and upbringing was fighting it. If someone knocked out this cornerstone of my belief, how much of me would crumble?

Mia shrugged and sat next to me on the couch. Her arm pressed into mine, and like before, it sent a thrum of soothing energy through me. "That's what I mean," she said. "It didn't stick."

Thac let out a small puff. A sigh of relief if I had to guess.

Mia was staring at her feet. "I met the other Valkyries though. One of them is sisters with a dragon, and two of the others are dating dragons."

I don't want to hear anything about I don't believe in vampires, *because I don't believe in vampires, but I believe in my own two eyes, and what I saw is fucking vampires!* Thank you, George Clooney and Quentin Tarantino for that memory. Replace *vampires* with *magic* and I'd have my life right now.

"To summarize, he's a god." I nodded at Thac. "And Mia has magical warrior queen friends who know dragons, and she's just good with it."

"It really changes one's perspective on the world," Mia said. "But isn't it epic?"

I'd been so focused on it being anti-everything I was raised on, that I was refusing to listen to a younger, less indoctrinated me who thought exactly that. "It is pretty epic. But if I'm a dragon, how do I keep myself from doing what I just did? Or at least, how do I get a say in when it happens?"

"I can call Magnus. Or Azzie. Ooh, probably Astrid, she was friendly. See if her boyfriend can help you."

"No." Thac laid the single word down like a hammer.

I probably shouldn't make another Thor reference. He didn't seem to care for those.

The look Mia gave him was frustration blended with disgust. "What is your problem?"

"I'm worried about you." His answer came without hesitation. While I believed he meant it, it felt as though another layer hid underneath. "Odin is stalking you. Other beings are—" He clamped his jaw shut. "You must be careful whom you trust."

"Scarlett is my best friend. She trusted me with her Valkyrie secret. I can give her a similar courtesy."

"Is she the one dating the dragon?" Thac asked.

"No. She's with a berserker. And Pan."

Pan, as in Greek God? Goat legs? Played a flute? Why was I at all surprised at this point?

"How do you know you can trust the others? You just met these women, and you don't know their mates." Thac was really pushing this hard.

I didn't blame him, but my reasons were probably a little different. I'd hurt anyone who went after Mia.

Her friends were hers to pick, though. It would be nice if whoever helped me was an actual help. "Could we not play guessing games or have political arguments or whatever this is, when it comes to me getting answers? I'd like to not go through this again." There would come a point where I couldn't control the rage, and if I was a dragon, who knew what kind of havoc that would wreak?

"I know one of the actual dragons." The hint of derision in Thac's voice was worse than if he'd been outright haughty. "I will call her. I will get you answers."

Swell. I liked the sound of that. "How long will this take, and what do we do until then?"

"She will answer when she answers." Thac made it sound like that was a reasonable reply.

Mia turned on the couch to face me, and covered my hand with hers. "We're here for you until then."

Her tone, her nearness, were more soothing than I thought possible. In fact, each time she brushed her fingers over my skin, I swore a soft voice murmured to the fury in my head, and the beast quieted. Even worse—better?—each of those soft touches was electricity sliding over my nerve endings. Drawing my desire to the surface. Reminding me of the *discovery* I did with Thac earlier. Making me want Mia naked and beneath me.

That was definitely the worst. I shouldn't want any of that. At all. Not in the midst of this confusion.

"Does Mia's father know who you are, Thac?" Open mouth, insert foot. Great way to distract everyone and make the situation even more tense, me. "And while we're on it, why does a god work as an enforcer for a crime boss?"

If Thac clenched his jaw any tighter, he might start cracking teeth.

"Does he?" Mia asked.

"While we're on the subject, what else are you hiding from her?" And now I was demanding answers from a god. One who could make it rain inside and probably literally strike me down with lightning if I pushed too hard.

Thac's silence was a raging roar of an answer. "I did promise you answers," he finally said.

FOURTEEN
MIA

I FELT THAC'S ANSWER IN MY GUT BEFORE HE SAID A word—yes, my father knew. There was a reason accepting this had all come easily to me.

I didn't know where the feeling came from, why I expected this cornerstone of my life to be yanked from under me, but I was certain a piece of the foundation my world was built on was about to crumble.

"Unlike you, there are things I can't say." Thac had that same tone of measuring his words that I'd come to expect from him whenever he discussed my father's business. Today things hit differently though. "And there are others that it's not my place to say, but I've felt for a long time like you deserve to know."

"Answer the questions." It took more strength than I thought to push the words past my abruptly dry throat. "What else are you hiding from me? Does Dad know what you are?"

"Caleb is right." Thac's nostrils flared. "I don't work for your father, we work with each other. It's more of a partnership."

Not what I expected, and I tried to make the pieces fit into the picture I was already forming. Into the information I had about my dad's life. "So you… what? Extort people? Are you in charge of… the gun ring?" Sometimes my mind wandered over what my father was dealing in, what type of illegal activities, but I always refused to follow the thought. Knowing made me complicit. Made me have to choose between him and what was right.

And until now, I'd convinced myself it was okay to ignore whatever the truth was.

Did Dad count on that? Did Thac?

"Ronan helps displaced magical beings find new homes," Thac said.

My mind snagged as reality and the world in my head collided and both fractured. There were so many things to unpack in that simple statement. "Does he extort them in exchange for his help?"

"No. Like any fae, a favor requires a price, but he keeps his request reasonable. He never asks for more than they can give without sacrifice."

This was harder to deal with than Scarlett telling me she had wings. This was… "Fae. As in faeries? But Dad told me… He let me think… Am I fae? He let me believe he was a crime lord."

"What he does *is* a crime in the place he came from." Thac delivered the words with a kind of softness, a kindness, that was unusual for him. "And your mother was human. You were born with her same traits."

Same traits. As in *you don't have a lick of magic.* "I..." I what? I was so fucking confused. "I need to talk to my father." Fortunately, he was immediately next door. Because we could walk into a doorway in Albany, and step out into St. Louis in a blink.

"Please, let me explain." Thac grabbed my arm, his fingers digging in enough to make an impression. Any other circumstance, and I'd think that was hot. I'd want him tossing me onto the couch and doing whatever came next.

He was a fucking god. My father was a faerie.

I was still nothing.

I jerked out of Thac's grip, and walked out of his condo.

He followed, and so did Caleb.

"Maybe he's right. You should learn more—"

I glared over my shoulder at Caleb, silencing him. "I am going to learn more. From the man who knows why he kept all of this from me, not from a third party."

"Stop. We'll talk. I'll answer your questions." Thac's tone implied he thought I would do exactly what he said.

Nu-uh. Not today. "I want answers from the man who lied to me my entire fucking life. The man who asked you to lie to me. I thought… I thought…"

I didn't know what I'd thought. Or why Thac was trying to stop me. I didn't know much of anything anymore.

My father was a horrible person committing horrible crimes, who I loved anyway. He let me believe that about him. Plus, he told me magic wasn't real. The fact that I put those two things at the same level of *terrible lie* said bad things about me, I was sure.

But I'd always known he couldn't really hurt people. That he had reasons for doing what he did. For a long time, I worried I was that delusional. I was convincing myself he was a better man than he really was.

Ronan helps displaced magical beings find new homes. It's a crime where he comes from.

What the fuck?

He even raised me with the same rules he grew up with. And watched me ooh and ahh over my comics. Over superheroes. Over fictional beings who could do magic. And never once told me *at least some of that is real.*

I'd had to learn from my best friend. At least Scarlett understood how important it was for me to know. But my own father…

I walked into his building, never pausing. Thac and Caleb tried to join me on the elevator, but an invisible wall seemed to lay between us. They looked like huffing, grumpy mimes, pressing into a barricade I couldn't see as the doors closed between us.

The car took me alone up to Dad's office, and he was waiting for me when I stepped off.

"Mia. I didn't realize you were in town." He studied me with a friendly gaze.

No hug though. Odd.

Not that he got a hug today. Not until I had answers. "Who are you?" I asked. "And while we're on it, who am I, and was my mother even the woman you claim she was?"

"Your mother was every bit the woman I've told you about. She was incredible. Brilliant. Fierce. I've never loved anyone the way I loved her." Emotion slid into his reply, the way it always did when he talked about Mom. "And you are every bit her daughter." He gestured to his office. "Sit with me. Talk."

I didn't realize I was waiting for him to rest his hand on the small of my back and nudge me, until he walked ahead of me and sat behind his desk.

Fine. Always be polite, even in severe circumstances. I took the seat across from him. "When you say every bit her daughter, does that also mean *painfully human*?" I asked.

"As opposed to…?"

"I don't know. A god. A faerie. A fucking unicorn?"

Dad raised his brows. "I promise you neither you nor your mother is something as dangerous as a unicorn. How long have you known?"

"About magic? About it being real?" It made sense that he'd ask me similar questions to the ones I was demanding he answer, but the same instinct that had told me all this time that I was finally learning the truth was insisting now that I not give all of the same to him. Maybe it was spite over his big lie, or perhaps it was something else, but I didn't want to tell him about the Valkyries. Especially since I didn't have to. "Scarlett is dating a god. And a berserker. Unlike you, she didn't hide it from me."

The sound Dad made was half-grunt, half-sigh. "I was fae. Technically I still am, but I'm not allowed to call myself that. When I fell for your mother, when I chose her over the court, I was exiled and branded an elf. Because you're half-human, you were born an elf. Without magic, if they ever come for you, or for me and want to hurt me, they will go through you. That's why I kept it a secret—to keep you safe."

"That is like the most bullshit explanation ever. Straight out of a bad book." I couldn't believe what I was hearing. *"To keep me safe?"*

"Have you seen what your friend's lovers can do?" Dad asked.

Scarlett's story about the fight against Odin

rushed back. About the things Arnlaug did. Pan. About allies bringing an entire mountain down around the god. "I have an idea."

"If you truly have an inkling of what's out there, you realize that if some of those creatures are my enemies, that's dangerous. Especially since you don't…" Dad clenched his jaw.

Since I didn't have magic. "I still can't believe… My entire life… Did you think I'd grow old and die, never knowing? That I'd just peacefully fade away and you'd rob me of that one piece of knowledge that I've wanted so desperately for so long?"

"I did hope, yes. I did what was best for you."

Said by every person ever who took another person's agency from them. "No. You did what was convenient for you."

"I made hard choices, Mia." An edge slid into his voice.

He was getting upset with *me*? Frustration crackled over my skin, and sparked in my mind. "You took away my right to choose for myself."

"I can't lose you. Not like I did…" Dad clenched his jaw.

Not like he lost Mom. Not something we talked about often, but I always felt his grief under the surface of all our conversations.

And I understood that feeling, though I didn't remember her. I missed the mother I'd never known. I stood. "That's not a reason for keeping something like this from me. That's all there is to it."

"Mia, please try to understand." My father's words landed against my back as I walked out the door.

Was this why Kirby couldn't make me into a Valkyrie? New questions rolled into my mind as I rode the elevator down, trying to squash the hurt. Trying to distract me from the way my reality was turning to rubble. Could she not gift me with the power because I was human with fae blood? Because I was an elf just for being born?

Were there rules like that?

I might know if I'd been filled in on this before… oh, *now*.

I can't lose you. The grief in my father's words drilled into me, as much as I didn't want to acknowledge any of it. He had his reasons, but the impact his choice made on me…

When I reached the lobby, I barely glanced at Caleb and Thac where they waited. I couldn't stay in this building anymore. I didn't know how to process the deception.

As I reached the street, they caught up to me. What was I supposed to do? What did I want to do?

The only thing I knew was I had to get away from here.

"Talk to me, Mia." Thac stepped in my path.

I wasn't sure I could even do that. I forced my

gaze to his, because I wouldn't cower from this truth. "Why didn't you tell me before today?"

"Ronan asked me not to." Thac's answer came without hesitation. Finally. "He didn't make me take an oath or anything, but he said it was dangerous for you to know. He's my friend, and he's been there for me for centuries. I owe him a lot."

"But you told me today."

Thac nodded. "Because you've become my friend too." Did he falter on the word *friend*? "It impacts you, and you deserve to know."

Why was that enough from him and not from dad?

Because Dad wasn't sorry. He didn't see what he'd done wrong. And he was the reason Thac had even considered keeping the secret. "I can't be here. Please?" The fight was draining from me fast, and I just wanted to break. I wouldn't do it in front of Dad's building, and I'd rather not do it in front of Thac and Caleb, but I may not have a choice.

"We'll go someplace else. The other side of the world." Caleb pointed me toward the doorway we came through earlier. "Those doors go anywhere, right?"

"Not unless you know how to use them," Thac said.

Of course. "Which I don't, because I was never told…" Damn it.

Thac placed his hand on the door. "I know a place. I have a place."

Thank God—literally apparently—because I needed to escape and put my head back on straight.

Not that doing so would stop my entire life from being a lie.

FIFTEEN
THAC

A LOUD CAW, LIKE A RAVEN, SPIT THE AIR. AN UNUSUAL sound in the middle of the city, and it drew my attention as a black blur dove at us from the sky.

This wasn't a bird, though. The closer the shape grew, the more clear it became we were looking at something humanoid in size and shape.

Instinct kicked in, and before my mind caught up, I was summoning a gust of stiff wind to push the attacker back. The same dense air acted as a shield between us and it.

Caleb stepped between Mia and the attacker, in a fighting stance reminiscent of a blend of martial arts. Mia had her hands up and fists balled, like she was ready to box.

Neither approach would do us any good, but at least they were prepared.

The magic in the air grew heavy, like syrup. This

time as the attacker headed toward us, I saw a face. A woman with piercing blue eyes and blond hair, and she wore intricate armor.

Valkyrie armor.

And she was wielding a flaming sword.

She circled us to come from behind, and seemed to be targeting Mia.

Caleb's arm had turned dragonoid again, and his wings were back. As our attacker drew closer, and I worked out how to best repel her without hurting the others, Caleb swung both arm and wing, and an invisible wave pushed the woman—the Valkyrie—away from us.

She circled back to attack from a third angle, and sliced at Mia with the sword.

The scream Mia let out curdled my blood and sent my rage soaring. I wrapped the Valkyrie in wind and ice, spinning her and freezing her wings at the same time. Flame shot from Caleb's hands, crackling and hissing as it met my icy attack.

The Valkyrie screamed, and landed several meters away, stumbling and struggling to find her balance.

With our attacker down for the count, and a nasty burn running down Mia's left arm, we needed to get to safety.

"Move. Now." I barked the order, and wrapped an arm around Mia's waist. There was a fine line between helping her hurry and picking her up and carrying her, and I managed to ride it and do both with an urgency that was less helpful than it could've been.

But we were on the other side in a few seconds, a door between us and the threat. The balmy air wrapped around us, chasing away the chill of Missouri and of the fight.

"Did we just walk out of a closet?" Mia turned to stare at the doorway we'd walked through.

Caleb was focused on the rest of the room. "Man, I thought I came out of the closet years ago."

"We will be safe here until we have more answers and a plan." First though, Mia needed our attention. "There are bandages in the bathroom. A green glass bottle about the size of a fist, with a cork stopper. Grab those," I said to Caleb. "I'll get some rags and we'll clean the area. Mia, you sit."

She raised her brows, but sank onto the edge of the bed without a word. I helped her peel off her jacket so as to not further injure her arm.

Caleb returned to the room the same time I did, with the requested jar in hand.

"This is going to sting," I said to Mia as I knelt on the floor, next to where she sat. "Give me your arm."

She did so without argument. Again.

Now that we had a moment to think, I examined the burn with a more critical eye. It was a straight line, the way a well-wielded blade should mark, but it didn't look like a cut. The flesh wasn't destroyed, but it was all burned.

That must mean Mia got out of the way before the flaming blade did real damage. Something about the explanation didn't make sense, but I was looking at proof, so it must be reality.

Caleb helped with cleaning and dressing the wound, not just obeying my directions, but reacting as if he anticipated each new request. He'd done this before, and the synchronicity with which we moved together was a pocket of calm in this bizarre situation.

"Look at me. Getting patched up by two hot guys." Mia's joke sounded more like the woman I knew, but her tone was flat.

"Not sure if I want to be where you are, or stay where I am," Caleb teased.

Mia almost smiled. "Being here means you're the one with the injury."

Caleb sucked his teeth. "True. You probably already know this, but playing doctor is a lot more fun when no one starts off hurt."

They both laughed, then fell silent within seconds.

I couldn't imagine what was going through their minds, but I suspected it was chaotic. I didn't have much comfort to offer beyond *at least you know the truth now,* so I finished wrapping Mia's arm in silence.

I stood and offered Mia a hand. I pulled her to her feet as Caleb straightened as well.

"My home is yours, as long as you're here and any

time you're here," I said. "Should we move to someplace with better seating for three?"

"How old are you?" Mia asked as we settled in the living room.

"I stopped counting at a thousand years, and calendars have changed many times over the centuries."

The laugh she let out was strangled and disconcerting. "How old is my dad?"

It was impossible to miss Mia's mood. Caleb's hesitance as he processed.

I had no idea how to help either but to tell them whatever I could. I only wished I didn't have to hide what Ronan had told me about Kirby. "My answer is the same. I've known him longer than I have the Espaniols."

Mia twisted her mouth.

Caleb let out a long whistle. "And now you're stuck babysitting."

I didn't care for the term or what it implied, I also didn't like Mia's frown. She seemed more bothered by the information her father had withheld than the fact that Kirby had attacked us in the open, in the middle of St. Louis.

"You're not babies," I said. "You've lived lives that come with a great deal of experience, and you've matured along the way. My having lived more of those experienced years doesn't mean I think of you as animals or helpless children."

"There's so much we haven't seen. So much we don't know," Mia wore a scowl I wanted to wipe away and never see return.

If she only saw that reality the same way I did. "Of course there is. There will always be new experiences—life would get boring otherwise. Every century, every decade, every year, I have to learn things I didn't know before. I get to experience things I've never seen before. Learning and growth don't cease when one hits a certain age. There's no cut-off line where an individual says that's it, I'm done, there's nothing more for me to know."

When that happened, the individual didn't usually last long after. I mourned those friends I'd lost that way, and a cloud of sadness settled in at their memories.

I shook the thoughts away.

"Are all immortals as wise as you?" Caleb asked.

"There's no bar that measures levels of wisdom. Like anyone else, different immortals know different things and grow at different weights." However, I did know what he was asking. "For instance, Jackass was created by beings older than I am."

The edges of Mia's expression softened. "The TV show?"

"Makes sense. Mortals don't walk away from that shit unscathed." Caleb seemed to finally be sinking into acceptance.

"But… those people have aged over time, haven't

they?" Mia asked. "They seem older now than they did when the show started."

"They do appear that way, yes," I confirmed. They may be a group of immortals with a penchant for the ludicrously dangerous, but they understood the things that were an actual risk to them—the wrong kind of cult following, for instance.

"Most diplomatic answer ever. When you're not…" Caleb trailed off.

Mia studied him. "When he's not what?"

I was curious as well. Also grateful she seemed to be climbing from her foul mood.

Caleb looked between us. "When he's not letting his concern for you drive him into a near rage, he's downright polite."

Of course I was. There was no call to be unreasonable unless the situation required otherwise. Mia going missing required a different level of urgency.

Pink spread across Mia's cheeks, complimenting and shifting her beauty. "What next?" She asked. "What attacked us on the street? What do we do about the fact that Caleb sets things on fire by mistake and grows a tail without warning."

"Kirby attacked us on the street." I could answer one question easily, though I wished it was the one thing I didn't understand.

Especially when Mia's scowl returned. It was different this time. More angry and less hurt. "That wasn't Kirby."

"When there were dozens of Valkyries, few had black wings." I didn't know much about them, but it was my understanding black was an indication of a Valkyrie with a killer's soul. "Are there more now?" Was Kirby creating all of her warriors to destroy?

Mia shook her head. "As far as I know, Kirby's the only Valkyrie with black wings, but there have to be other creatures with that feature. Is that a fair assumption?"

"That is true." The harder I pushed, the more she would resist the truth. I was furious with myself for letting her vanish to Greece with this Kirby woman, and for completely missing that Mia had almost been turned under my watch, so I needed to figure out quickly how best to show her she'd put her faith in the wrong individual.

"Besides, that wasn't a person." Caleb's statement, his certainty about it, caught me off-guard. "Rather, it was someone who could take a non-human form."

"How do you know that?" I asked.

Caleb shrugged. "I don't know. I just do. Did you not both see it? If anything was a dragon, it was what attacked us."

This was unraveling in ways I was unfamiliar with. "I hope Artura calls us back soon." I hadn't meant to speak the thought aloud.

"That's what I've been saying." Caleb sounded frustrated.

"I hope so too." Mia sighed and stood. She

wobbled on her feet and immediately sank back to the couch.

I didn't like the look of that. "Are you all right?"

She pressed her palm to her forehead. "Just a little dizzy. It must've been a longer day than I thought." Her speech was slower, too. Not noticeable, not like a drunk Mia, but it wasn't filled with her normal strength.

"You should get some sleep." I wasn't going to argue about this. "You can stay in the bedroom."

"Is that an order?" One corner of her mouth pulled up.

I nodded. "Go lay down. Sleep. Any plan we make will be more effective if we're rested, and we're safe here, so that can happen. And we won't reveal any more secrets while you rest."

"Does that mean there are more secrets to reveal?" Mia asked.

Only the one, and it wasn't information I could give her. "I do hope not."

Caleb and I left Mia to sleep. I wasn't sure about continually finding myself alone with him. Largely because I wasn't sure how to feel about him. This intriguing, attractive man who was a dangerous combination of compelling and unknown threat.

"Now what?" Caleb asked.

"You're welcome to do whatever you'd like. I'm going to sit outside by the water and spend some time collecting my thoughts." I needed my own version of rest.

"May I join you?"

"Only if you stay silent."

Caleb pulled his fingers across his mouth and sealed his lips shut.

I would assume that was agreement. I headed down to the water and made myself comfortable in the sand. He settled next to me.

For a little while, I struggled to find my center with his presence so close. However, when he remained silent, settling into a more relaxed state of mind became easy.

I watched as the sun set over the ocean. In this meditative state, I was aware of the world around me, but it was background noise, as was the passage of time. The water lapped at the sand a few meters away, the stars came out to play above our heads, and at some point Caleb lay back.

None of it required more than acknowledgement and appreciation because it was all beauty and no danger.

When Mia's steps whispered in the sand behind us, drawing me from the deeper state. The sky was growing light again, as we crept toward morning. She sat between Caleb and me, waking him up, and causing him to push into a drowsy half-sitting position.

"Thank you for telling me the truth and for

looking out for me." Her soft voice wove with the beauty rather than disrupting it.

I will be here for the whole of your existence. "Only for you," I said aloud.

"Really? Never anyone else? For more than a thousand years?" Caleb asked in disbelief.

Why did he choose now to speak? "There have been others I've cared about deeply. Each of them is gone."

"That's a sobering thought." Mia pulled her legs to her chest and rested her chin on her knees.

SIXTEEN
THAC

THIS TIME THE SILENCE WAS UNCOMFORTABLE. RATHER than something that could be meditated to.

"I saw a chessboard inside. Do you play?" Caleb shattered the silence.

I didn't know why he'd asked such a ridiculous question, but I was grateful for the change of subject. "Why would I have it if I didn't intend to use it?"

"Because it's also a gorgeous piece of art?" Caleb said.

That was a fair point. "It is attractive. The pieces are hand carved stone. But there's no reason to own it if I don't play."

Caleb seemed to consider this. "Then you can play the piano in there as well."

"Yes."

"Thac's the one who taught me to play chess."

Hearing Mia join the conversation was a relief. Her tone was neutral.

Caleb adjusted his position in the sand, putting him in front of us, making it easier for all three of us to look each other in the eye. "Seriously?" Caleb asked. "You're so good I just… I figured you'd been playing forever. One of those instances of head of the chess club in high school. Kicking everyone's ass. Known in top secret underground chess circles around the world…" His voice was filled with affection.

And the pink that spread across Mia's face was enhanced in light of the rising sun. She and Caleb were more to each other than two people sharing a house.

"I was also certain you knew already. You're a natural at the game, and I wondered if you'd let me teach you out of some misplaced sense of respect," I said.

"Does that sound like me?" Mia asked.

It did not. "No."

"I prefer not to do most things I did in high school." A shadow darkened her eyes. "Which is why I like the chess." Like that, she was back to neutral.

"Is this the part of the movie where our intrepid heroes take a pause to share their tragic pasts?" Caleb teased.

Mia rapidly shook her head. "No. That's a bad idea on so many levels."

I agreed that dwelling in the past was rarely helpful, though I doubted her reasons were the same as mine. "Why is that?"

"Because in the movies, if the heroes all pause to get to know each other, it means they're about to start dying. Gotta drum up sympathy for them before you kill them off." Mia made the concept sound like the most reasonable assumption.

The sounds of morning birds darting through the waters were an eerie soundtrack to her statement.

"You're the final girl, though." Caleb seemed as into this concept as Mia. "You don't die. It's one of us."

This was sobering. "None of us is going to die."

"No, not actually." The sigh Mia let out was exaggerated. "But it's more fun to pretend that than focus on the reality. If we're sharing our sordid pasts, I vote someone besides me goes first."

I wanted to make something about this situation better for her. Anything to get her smile to stay longer than a few seconds. To make her joy genuine. "We would be here for a while if I told you about all of my past, but if you ask me anything, I'll share. However the memory is at the surface of your mind now. If it haunts you this way, sharing among friends may help."

Mia pressed her forehead to her knees, hiding her face. For a moment, she was still. The scent of the ocean and the crash of the waves filled in the lack of conversation.

"I didn't go to a normal public or private school." Her words were muffled until she looked up again. "Dad decided it was safer for me to work with private tutors, so I don't have that experience to draw on. But I do have what I saw on TV, and back then there was nothing I wanted more than to be a part of something like that."

"It's not all it's cracked up to be," Caleb said softly.

"I've heard stories since, but back then I just wanted to be around people who..." Mia puffed out her cheeks and pushed out a large sigh.

I didn't want to see her stuck in whatever type of memory this was. This Mia was withdrawn and sad and I didn't know how to help. "You don't have to tell us this." I shouldn't have nudged her to do so in the first place.

"I know. But you're right—getting it out might help. It might not, but I'm not living the experience again, so I doubt it will hurt more." Mia drew her hand down her face. "I also had bodyguards everywhere I went. Big, tough, muscled and tattooed. The kind of men most people look at and cross the street to get away from."

"One of them looked a lot like..." Mia pursed her lips. "Doesn't matter. He was head of my security detail when I was fourteen and fifteen. He loved to remind me that I was only special because of who my father was. That I was tall and fat and no man was ever going to want what I had to offer." Like that, Mia's voice went cold and emotionless.

"But not in those words. Never directly. He was more subtle about it. Things like pointing out gorgeous women on the street and comparing me to them. Reminding me every time I had something sweet or an extra serving or a side of dressing…"

Fury raced through me. This was her past, so I didn't need to act now, but when her story was done, I'd find this man, and I'd carve her anguish across his soul until he felt nothing else, for eternity.

The light vibration that ran from Caleb's clenched fists up his arms said I could count on him to help.

Mia wasn't looking at us, though. She stared into the distance, past the water line. "I thought he was right, so it wasn't as though I complained or bit back. Right before I turned sixteen, he tried to…"

If he had touched her, his suffering would be worse when I found him.

Caleb bumped her lightly with his shoulder. "You don't have to."

"It's not anything like what you're thinking. Okay, it's probably a little like what you're thinking, but not." Mia fiddled with her lips, nearly chewing her fingernails, but not quite. "He told me that he was willing to show me what it was like to be with a man, since I wasn't ever going to find out on my own. But I had to get Dad to pay him more first. Because spear fishing for whales was illegal and he wasn't taking that risk without a little extra reward." Her voice cracked, and her eyes shone with unshed tears. "The way he laughed…"

My growl slipped out, and I couldn't—didn't want to—rein it back in.

She glanced at me. Through me. "Dad found me crying in my room." Mia dragged in a shaky breath, and most of her emotion vanished. "He made me tell him what had happened. I didn't tell him all of it, only about the conversation that day. I didn't know the rest of it was bad—I thought I deserved it. Anyway, Dad told me it had been taken care of, and I never saw the guy again. I heard whispers in the halls. Nothing concrete, but enough that I put together Dad was a powerful man. I'd seen the movies. The Sopranos. I knew what *made him pay* and *used his connections* meant."

If Ronan had taken care of this man, I didn't need to do anything. But I still wanted to hunt the asshole down, and rip his windpipe out with my bare hands for ever daring to say anything like that to Mia.

"I don't suppose it meant what I thought after all," Mia said.

One of the reasons I liked Ronan, that we'd gotten

along for so many years, was he dispensed justice in a similar way to my blessings. "Fae deal in favors and luck. And some luck is very bad." I searched for a comparable analogy. "As in, God cursed Job bad. Ronan doesn't have to do anything himself except wish the appropriate luck on the person who wronged him. Or you, in this case. Happenstance takes care of the rest."

"Anyway." Mia's sadness evaporated. "I got some better friends after that. Not on purpose. I happened to meet someone who was good to me because they were a good person. I really have dealt with most of that… sort of. But sliding into it is hard, so let's not linger there."

I wanted to wrap her up and make sure the memory never haunted her again, but there was nothing for me to do except be honest with her. I hated that she'd suffered through that. Did Ronan have any idea what cost his decisions held for Mia? "He was wrong. I hope you know that. You're the kind of beauty that haunts dreams and drives good men to madness."

"For a thick girl? For a chubby chick?" Bitterness filled Mia's retort.

"For a gorgeous woman," Caleb said. "No qualifiers. He's right, you're more than stunning."

"You truly are." I wouldn't let him steal my lines, and in the peace of this place, I couldn't let myself ignore the pull to Mia any longer.

Mia let out a flat chuckle. "Then why do you tease me so much? Why do you keep me at arm's length?"

Her anguish pierced my heart. "Because with you, I can't act on what I feel."

"Why not?" Two words. One simple question. Yet, she was asking for an answer that was far more complex than it seemed on the surface.

Or was it really that complicated? My because… died on my lips.

"He's going to tell you it's because of your dad." Caleb's easy answer made me growl mentally.

I didn't dare confirm, but he was right.

Mia sighed and shook her head. "Guess what? Despite what my dad thinks, I'm my own person. He doesn't own me."

"I realize that." I did. Those weren't just words. "But he is a friend."

"Is Caleb a friend?" Mia asked.

I looked the other man over with a *not really* pushing to get out. But that wasn't accurate. "I suppose." Friend might not be the right word, but he was becoming more than an acquaintance.

"Thanks for the vote of confidence, dude." Sarcasm bled from Caleb's words. "But I suppose it's fair."

"If Caleb told you to keep your hands off me, would you?" Mia asked.

So that was where this was going. She would logic me into a corner, and I would concede her point. At least losing this argument meant I finally got to taste her. *Creation* I'd wanted that for so long. "No. If Caleb told me to keep my hands off you, I wouldn't listen to him."

"Am I a friend?" This time Mia spoke with a timidness I hated seeing in her. After her story about her teenage years, I understood why.

I nodded. "Without question."

"If I told you there are nights I lie awake fantasizing about you pinning me down… I press my vibrator between my legs, but it's still not you, and I know it, and God I want you there instead…" Mia's words came out rushed, and she stared at the sand as she trailed off.

My cock strained against my trousers, roaring for what I'd denied myself for so long. Demanding I give Mia what she wanted.

If I spoke, if I moved, if I did anything besides sit here frozen like a coward, I'd act on the impulses.

"If I told you I'm not asking for forever, that I just want a little taste." I was tired of holding back. My answer to her was to kneel in front of her in the sand, tunnel my fingers in her hair, and look her in the eye. "Never doubt that like the piano, like the chess set, you're a beautiful piece of art, that I want nothing more than to run my fingers over. Again and again. To play your body until your voice rewards me with the most beautiful music."

"Then what's stopping you?" There was a

pleading in her question, a pull in her gaze, that I couldn't ignore.

I crushed my mouth to hers.

Mia whimpered against my lips.

Caleb groaned.

I may regret this later, but I doubted it.

SEVENTEEN
MIA

I'D NEVER BEEN KISSED LIKE THIS BEFORE. THERE WAS AN intensity spilling from Thac that muddled my mind and made my pulse race. I couldn't press close enough, but I needed more. I needed him. I needed this to last forever.

When Caleb groaned, I couldn't pretend I'd forgotten he was here. I hated to do it, but I pushed Thac away enough to ask, "What about Caleb?"

"He can leave, or he can watch. I'd be happy if he joined us, but that's up to the two of you." The gravel in Thac's voice was as delicious as the rest of this.

If I could focus on desire, on his touch, nothing else would matter for at least a little while. Not the secrets or my past or any of it. I met Caleb's gaze and saw desire reflected back at me.

He crawled toward us, and brushed his mouth

along the edge of my ear. "Tell me to go, and I will." His hot whisper teased my skin.

"Don't go." I turned my head enough to kiss him, too. His mouth was different. Still hard. Still demanding, but Thac tasted like eternal safety and Caleb was abandon and chaos.

I wanted both.

The story from my past still lingered in my mind. Both more and less potent than if I'd kept it to myself. The part I didn't tell them was how much time I'd spent chasing the assurance that I was desirable. How many people I'd fucked to convince myself I wasn't a bog witch.

I'd learned from that, too. I didn't tend to seek validation in sex anymore, but with Thac, with Caleb, they'd each been temptations in their own way for so long...

I forced my mind to be silent, and leaned into Caleb's fingers dancing up my back while Thac yanked my hair and probed my mouth with his tongue.

From there, Thac dragged a series of kisses down my jaw and along my neck. He seemed intently focused on tasting every inch of my skin between my mouth and my collar.

Caleb's touch was more playful, but no less attentive. He glided his hands over my clothing, pinching and teasing, brushing my bra, then sliding underneath fabric.

I'd been with two men at the same time before, but it wasn't anything like this. That was a frat party I'd found myself at, and I was pinned between two best friends. It was more groping and getting poked than anything, and when it was all over, I got the distinct impression it had been more about the conquest and bragging rights than anything else.

Mostly I thought that because when it was over, one said to the other *Told you she'd go for it. Pay up.*

This was nothing like that, and the way Thac dropped his kisses lower the instant Caleb tugged my shirt up, made the vile memory fade. Caleb tossed aside my top and unhooked my bra, managing tender and desperate at the same time.

Instinct wanted me to cover up and hide, rather than sitting on a beach, exposed.

Thac raked his gaze over me with a look no one had ever turned on me before, and his hungry touch sent shivers of want spilling through me. He lowered his mouth, wrapped his tongue around one of my nipples, and drew it in to suck and nibble. The way he kneaded my breasts and the intensity in his attentions made desire clench in my gut.

At the same time, Caleb pulled me into him, stealing my balance. Stealing my breath. Making it impossible to know which of them to touch. I couldn't reciprocate. I couldn't figure out which of their touches to focus on.

"I didn't think you liked me this way." I hadn't

meant for the insecurity to slip through, and I didn't know which of them I was talking to.

Both of them, really.

Caleb tugged at the edge of my ear with his teeth. "I've been telling you since I met you how much I want you."

Snippets of our past conversations flitted back, ending on just a few nights ago, watching Gremlins together. Joking about making me scream his name. Getting me wet. "I thought you were…"

"Joking?" Caleb danced his fingers down my stomach to undo my pants with a flick of his wrist. "No." He glided lower, over my trousers, to press his fingers into the seam. Into my dampening core. "I meant every single word of it."

Thac's growl hummed over me as he continued to devour me with kisses and nibbles. He nudged me onto my back. "He'd be an idiot to not want you. Gorgeous mind and body like yours?"

A self-depreciating retort stuck in my throat. *Are you sure you're talking about me? Are you drunk?*

But with the sand heating my bare skin, with Caleb kneeling next to me and Thac between my legs, I wanted to focus on now. Caleb slanted his mouth over mine in an all-consuming kiss. He tasted like the promise of eternity.

Thac tugged the rest of my clothing down my legs, exposing the rest of me. The way he dragged his fingers up the insides of my legs made me shiver in anticipation. When he traced a light touch over my already slick pussy, I groaned and squirmed.

The sighs escaping my chest became a squeal of surprise when Caleb pinned my hands above my head. I was trapped between him and Thac, and it was the hottest thing I'd ever experienced. Especially as Caleb used his free hand to roll my nipples between his fingers. As Thac drew his touch along my skin to slip two digits inside me.

Thac teased, pumping in and out. Moving faster, deeper, until my hips thrust in time to his touch. My disappointment when he withdrew was short-lived, as he glided up to my clit. He traced circles around the swollen nub, tightening the path until I couldn't think about anything else but how close I was to pleasure.

He kept pushing and desire mounted inside me.

When I came, waves of orgasm crashed around me, and the sounds of the ocean just a few feet away made me think of that need lapping at my mind. Pulling me into ecstasy.

Thac leaned forward to catch himself on his hands on either side of my head, and searched my face. "You're even more stunning when you're flushed with desire," he murmured, and dipped his head to brush his mouth over mine.

My skin was hot, my mind wanted more, and every inch of me felt like a live wire. I wanted one of them inside me, or both of them. At the same time, one after another…

Apparently this was making me greedy.

My thoughts weren't completely gone, though. "Condoms?"

Thac bit gently along my lips. "I don't get diseases. I won't get you pregnant unless you and I agree to it. I will wear one today, and we'll discuss it again when we're not both eager to rut."

Discuss it again? We'd do this more than once. He wanted to have me more than once.

My heart fluttered at the small but intense hint that he had that kind of desire for me.

"Some of us aren't that lucky." Caleb had already stripped off his shirt, and as he took off his pants, he paused long enough to grab two foil packets from his wallet.

Both men finished undressing, and Caleb stepped in to roll on their condoms. Watching him roll a rubber onto Thac's cock, seeing his teasing touch and hearing Thac's groan of desire, was delicious.

Thac knelt between my legs again, and nudged my opening with the head of his cock. He slipped inside me slowly, stretching me out and drawing out the penetration.

Fuck that felt incredible.

When he was buried inside, he sat that for a moment, twitching occasionally, but not moving. And then he leaned in, wrapped his arms around me, and pulled me upright with him, so I was straddling his lap. There was no strain in his posture. His breathing never increased. He was supporting my weight, hands on my ass and back, and slowly thrusting inside me.

God this felt incredible.

Caleb pressed into me from behind. There was another slow, long glide as he stretched out my opening further with his fingers. As he slipped his cock into me, against Thac's.

I had no idea how they both fit inside me, and it was almost uncomfortable, but it was also delicious. All-consuming.

They were kissing me again. Thac with his mouth on mine, and Caleb along my neck and shoulders. They were holding me. Cradling me between them like I was the most precious thing in the world.

The rocking of them inside me turned into a steady rhythm, and Caleb moved his hands back to my breasts. Thac sucked on the soft flesh of my neck, drawing the skin between his teeth and marking me over and over, as they fucked me slowly. Completely.

I was wrapped in so much pleasure, I lost track of it. I fell into a chasm of need. I was aware of the delicious sounds each man made as they came, and I'd never felt more safe, more wanted, as they slowed to a reluctant stop.

It took some maneuvering to separate, and we curled up around each other in the sand.

Laying on the beach with these two men who occupied so much of my mind and my life, wrapped in both of them as the sun caressed our bare skin, would be heaven for most. But me? I was waiting for the guilt that came with sex. That nagging, heavy feeling that would sit in the pit of my stomach and remind me I'd been with someone who didn't like me, just for a little bit of touch.

The way Thac traced a lazy path along my arm, and Caleb's soft breath on my chest didn't carry that feeling.

They both wanted to be here.

And despite everything I'd learned in the last several hours, I understood why there had been secrets, and there weren't anymore.

"Where's your mind at?" Caleb drew a light touch along my bottom lip.

I wanted to say *only here.* I desperately wanted that to be true. "Everywhere."

"Should we head inside," Thac sounded reluctant. "Wash off the sand and put both of your clothes in the wash?"

"You have a washing machine?" It was a stupid question. I'd seen all the modern tech Thac used—he didn't live differently than anyone else—but the thought popped into my head, and I wanted to grasp anything that wasn't a thought about me.

"One of the most important lessons I've learned is

that anything associated with modern plumbing is worth worshiping," Thac said.

Caleb scrunched up his face. "Noted. Also, is there a god of toilets?"

"I can think of several I'd call that, but I know of none who have claimed the title."

My laugh slipped out at Thac's joke. He was letting Caleb see his less-grumpy side. Should I be jealous that they were getting along? It seemed like yes, that feeling should be there.

But they both wanted me.

Was this real?

Yup. I was fucked up enough that I didn't question magic or being descended from fae or the existence of multiple gods, but I doubted that someone—two someones—wanted me for me. "Inside sounds good."

Thac pulled me to my feet with zero effort. Walking toward the bungalow wearing nothing, a gorgeous built man on either side of me, yanked forward *all* the self-consciousness. Neither of them seemed to mind their nakedness or mine though.

Thac led us to the side of the house, to a tightly packed clay pad surrounded by short trees with long leaves, and with a very modern looking removable shower head connected in the middle of it all. He turned on the water and tested the temperature before pointing the spray at us.

The next several minutes were spent washing

away the sand. There were a lot of roaming hands mixed into it all, with Caleb and Thac both giving me considerable attention, and sparing a little for each other as well.

This wasn't orgasmic, not like on the beach, but it was playful, and the longer they touched me, the more I was drawn into the fun, helping each of them wash sand off their backs. Their asses. Their cocks.

Kisses landed on my shoulders and neck. Light brushes of teasing fell along my thighs. Some of it tickled and most of it made me gasp in pleasure.

Neither man showed any sign of being bothered by my nakedness or the imperfections it revealed. I almost felt worshiped.

I was also reluctant to dry off, but the three of us even had fun patting towels over each other, before we headed inside.

Thac led us into the bedroom again. "We'll go back later for clothes for both of you. In the meantime, these should keep you comfortable." He handed me a T-shirt, and Caleb a pair of sweat shorts. "I'll be right back." Thac walked from the room with our other clothing.

I tugged on the shirt, and it fell about a third of the way down my thighs.

Caleb had to tie his shorts up tightly to keep them in place. He whistled with appreciation when he saw me, and a flush of heat raced through me. I'd never been cute in a guy's shirt before. Good first.

"If only Adam and Eve had woven cotton, huh?"

I got what Caleb meant—we almost looked like we were wearing the clothing version of fig leaves. Not literally, but what we were each trying to cover was similar.

"Hey, Thac, did you know Adam and Eve?" Caleb called.

Thac rejoined us. "I'm not that old, and I guarantee they weren't the people you think they were."

"Who does he think they were?" I asked.

"The mother and father of humanity."

Oh. I suppose that whole thing might play out differently once dragons and gods and the rest were involved. The thought looped back to all I'd learned in the past weeks, in the past few days, as we made ourselves comfortable in Thac's living room.

I was still mad at Dad for lying to me my entire life about who he was—who we were. The betrayal felt worse than when I thought I'd found out he was in crime. He let me think he was hurting people, because in the place he came from helping them was just as bad.

I sank into the cushions of an overstuffed sofa, and my heart skipped when Thac pulled me closer. Did he really want me around still?

I was tired of not knowing where I belonged, and the revelation from my father didn't help with that feeling. With the women in Greece, I swore I was almost there. I thought I was one of them.

Until Kirby showed me I was so ordinary, I couldn't even be given a magical power.

So this feeling with Thac and Caleb, this soothing that grew inside me and made me think I was where I should be when they were around, I couldn't trust it. On the beach, I told them that sex would be all physical—that was my promise. It wasn't what I wanted, but old habits died hard. And forming any longer term connection with either of them—one was a god and one was a dragon—wasn't in the cards for me.

Best to distance myself now, and work on healing the hurt before it got worse.

EIGHTEEN
CALEB

It was impossible to miss that Mia grew quieter as the minutes ticked away. Was she still lost in memories of the past she'd shared with us? That was something I understood all too well.

I pulled her legs onto my lap, and she didn't resist, though her smile didn't reach her eyes.

"We should head back to the real world soon," she said.

Thac drew a lazy line along her arm with his thumb. For months, every time I encountered the man, I'd only seen a big bruiser who radiated *don't fuck with me or mine*. But the last few days a more casual, caring side poke through.

Besides, he didn't seem to be a bruiser after all. "You wanted some time to think about everything you'd learned," He managed to sum up the chaos our lives had become in such a benign way, I would've laughed if there wasn't a gray cloud creeping in around us. "And we don't know where you're safe."

Mia furrowed her brow. "Right. Valkyries and mysterious attackers and..." She sighed, and straightened in her seat, pulling away from both of us as much as was possible, with the lack of space between us.

Did I miss something? Didn't we just have incredible sex on the beach? Playtime in the shower? I'd enjoyed the fuck out of the entire thing. Thac looked content. Mia fluctuated between a blank expression and one of misery.

Whatever caused this, I wanted to see her smile again. If her mood came from the dive into her past, I couldn't erase that, but I wanted to do *something.*

My gaze landed on what looked like a radio, on the narrow table against the wall. If I squinted, I almost swore I could see a light glow around the device, but that could just be the way morning light spilled into the room. "Is that a radio? Does it still work?"

"It is, and it does," Thac said. "However, it doesn't get regular stations. It's tuned to a magical frequency."

A shadow of a smile crossed Mia's face, but it vanished quickly under her impassive mask.

She was holding back, but not sadness. At least not as far as I could tell.

"May I?" I hated to extract myself from them, but

curiosity beckoned. I wandered toward the table, taking in the details of the little box as I got closer. The artfully crafted wood, that looked hand carved. The little knobs I realized as I got closer were dark brown instead of black. The asymmetrical imperfections were an indicator that they were shaped by hand as well, but the entire assembly was smooth and polished. "How do I…?"

"Right knob is volume. Left knob tunes it. It's not powered, and it's technically always on."

Following Thac's instructions, I searched for whatever a magical frequency would get me. With any luck, I wasn't about to find the god equivalent of talk radio. Such a thing had its place, but it wouldn't make things better here.

Music filtered through the speakers—a song and style I'd never heard before. It had similarities to modern pop, but the language was unfamiliar, the beat was reminiscent of Rush, and the chords made me think of Queen. What I caught of the lyrics made me think it was an upbeat song about hope.

I couldn't help but tap my feet. Sway my hips. Reach for Mia.

She grasped my fingers and sparks raced through me, electrifying my thoughts and heart. I pulled her up to join me, and this time her smile lingered. A glance at Thac showed his gaze following us, but he showed no sign or interest in joining.

That was fine with me—Mia was an incredible dance partner. She always loved to move, and she didn't hold back when she was enjoying the music. There was no pattern or reason to the way we danced, except to follow the beat, and the longer we moved, the more her sadness slipped away.

There had been a pull between us since the day I met her, and today that connection felt like the strongest of silk threads, binding us. With her in my arms, the joy whispering from her, everything felt like it could be right with the world, even a world I hadn't even begun to understand.

I could even watch her with Thac, as long as I got to be with her too. I had been anyway, the entire time I met her. The only thing I'd really been jealous about was that she had the big bruiser's attention. It would be easy to pretend now that I'd had that, I didn't want it after all, but I still did.

Did all of this feel more potent now? It was as if being together—the sex—had unlocked something. A bigger something than *sex good. Pretty lady mine.* This sensation ran deeper and felt older than just something basic and physical.

By the end of the second song, we were caught up in this rhythm, but talking replaced the music. I kissed the palm of her hand. Her fingertips. The gesture felt as natural as having her in my arms. As any of this.

"What are they saying?" Mia asked. "Their voice is so pretty."

I had to focus on the words to pluck any out, but the longer I listened the more I understood.

"I only ever learned enough fae to understand the swearing," Thac said.

"It's a top forty countdown." They were naming the song, the band, and hinting at what to expect next. "And a commercial for some sort of charm or spell?" At least, I assumed that MagiClean had a different meaning to magical beings than it did to humans.

Mia's hands tightened around mine, and then her gasp slipped completely. "Oh." She swayed on her feet.

I wrapped an arm around her waist to steady her, and she sagged against me.

"Are you all right?" I felt the pressure in the air change. It was heavier now. Not so fun-filled.

She straightened and pulled away from me. "I'm fine. I think it's been too long since I took my pills."

I led her back to the couch.

"What pills?" Thac asked.

A knock interrupted before she could answer, and he frowned. "Stay. Take it easy. I'll see who that is."

Did he get a lot of visitors in the middle of nowhere? This wasn't right. None of it. I wasn't sure how I knew that, but things had changed in the last few seconds.

"Artura." Thac's voice drifted in from the front door. He didn't sound upset or defensive—both tones I'd learned well in the last few days. "I'm honored to have you in my home."

That was definitely Thac deferring to his guest. Artura—wasn't the woman he was going to call about me being a dragon? I needed to see. I moved close enough to glimpse a woman with long, white hair. Height-wise, Thac dwarfed her by more than a foot, but even from here, it was clear she radiated a presence that consumed the space around her.

She looked up and her gaze met mine.

The wave of recognition that swept over me made me wobble on my feet the way Mia had moments ago.

"Oh, Skuld. What have you done?" The words she muttered weren't in English, but unlike the radio, I understood every word clearly.

I was crossing the room to her before I registered my feet were moving. The way she watched me radiated *are you real?* When I drew near enough, she reached for my hand.

Why did it feel like I'd known her my whole life? Longer. Was that possible? "Mother?" Why did I say that?

She grasped my fingers, and Thac's bungalow vanished. Thac vanished. Mia was gone.

Artura and I stood in a living room with bookcases lining the walls, and more books than they could ever hope to hold stacked on the coffee table and in piles by the chairs. By the door.

This was my dream living room.

"Where are we?" I asked.

She pressed a palm to my face, studying me. "I thought you were dead. All this time..."

NINETEEN
THAC

I DIDN'T UNDERSTAND MOST OF WHAT ARTURA SAID, BUT Caleb's *mother* was unmistakable. Was she the missing key I'd been looking for this entire time? It couldn't be.

But I'd just witnessed it.

Where did they go? Dragons could teleport, but why did she take him away from here?

"Where did they go?" Mia's question mirrored mine.

I turned to find her standing in the entryway behind me, her face pale, but her cheeks flushed bright red.

"I don't know," I said. "Artura took him." An obvious answer, but the only one I had.

"Bring him back." Mia cringed as the demand passed her lips. "Sorry. I don't know where that came from. But we need to get him. I need—" She swayed the way she had earlier.

I caught her before she hit the ground, and cradled her as I lowered us both to the floor. Her eyelids fluttered, but stayed closed and her neck was hot against my skin.

Caleb was the least of my concerns now. A whisper told me I cared, and I did. Mia looked to be in a more precarious situation than him, though.

The seconds that passed felt like an eternity before she regained consciousness and looked at me.

"What medication were you talking about?" I asked softly.

Her frown deepened. "For my condition."

Her…? "What condition?"

"The one I've had my whole life. I need my pills."

That wasn't a complete answer. "Should I call Ronan?"

"No." Mia scrambled to sit up, but it was like she was moving in slow motion.

This wasn't right. "If he has answers, it doesn't matter if you're mad at him. You just passed out."

"There's nothing for him to help with." The longer she spoke, the stronger her voice grew. "I just need the pills. This happens when I forget. There's no reason to involve him if we already have a solution."

I trusted her to know what she needed, but I didn't like the idea of leaving her alone. "Where are they? These pills?"

"Medicine cabinet in my bathroom at home. Only prescription bottle up there."

I could go and get those in a few minutes and be back. She was safe here. I scooped her into my arms and stood.

"What are you doing?" She wrapped her arms around my neck instead of trying to get away.

I carried her to my room. "You passed out. You're staying in bed until I return."

"I'm fine. Really."

I lay her on the mattress and fixed her with a stare. "Passing out is not *fine*. If you just need the pills, then once you take them, you can get out of bed."

Mia scowled. "But then we'll go get Caleb."

"And then we'll see how you feel. Caleb can take care of himself." I wasn't simply saying that to reassure her. From everything I'd seen recently, he was perfectly capable of it, and Artura wasn't a threat. She was an ancient and powerful being with no reason to pick on an individual. Especially if they were related.

The growl Mia let out was a familiar sound. She was going to argue. "A dragon just took him, according to you. How is he supposed to take care of himself?"

"Have some faith in him. We can't do anything yet regardless." I kissed her on the forehead. "I'll be back soon."

I expected her to argue at the brush-off, and she stood and grabbed my arm.

But her legs wobbled, and she collapsed onto the bed with a frown. "Hurry back," Mia said.

As I walked toward the doorway that would take me to the alley near her place, I muttered a series of spells to ward the house and keep her safe until I returned.

I stepped onto the street and cut a rapid pace toward Mia's. I had so many pieces, and they all felt like separate pictures—Caleb's heritage, Mia being offered the mantle of Valkyrie by a madwoman and being unable to accept—but I kept trying to jam them into the same image.

They were more connected than I could see. Instinct insisted as much.

Why couldn't I see how it all intertwined?

I let myself into Mia's, and headed for her medicine cabinet. As she'd said, there was a single prescription bottle among the handful of over-the-counter pills.

When I grabbed the bottle, a sharp jolt shocked me, and I dropped the container in surprise. *What in Creation's name?* I extracted the orange plastic vial from the sink, this time without incident.

Something wasn't right about these drugs though. A magic pulsed from them, thrumming gently against my skin. Sinking into my chest. Making my pulse skip in unpleasant ways. I pocketed the bottle, and the strange sensation softened, but didn't vanish.

I knew this magic. It was old and filled the air

with the taste of home. But a warped and twisted home. Why was Mia taking pills that radiated this kind of foulness?

Years ago, when I cut ties with Ronan, part of it was because of the company he kept. He'd been working with a group—a cult—who worshiped an imprisoned goddess of chaos and destruction.

There was a reason Malsumis had been locked away. While Ronan wasn't a believer, he hadn't understood at the time that her followers weren't to be trusted, regardless of what he hoped to get from the arrangement.

Had Mia really been ingesting these since she was a child? Did Ronan know? I didn't want to assume because this meant he was poisoning her in some way. Why?

He wouldn't hurt her—not Mia. Not his life and blood.

So why did Mia have these?

I needed to get back to her, but arriving without answers wouldn't help anyone. I had to talk to Ronan and see why she had these. What was wrong with her that such extreme measures were required?

My thoughts were a blur of questions as I returned to the doorway, stepped back onto the streets of St. Louis, and walked into Ronan's building. Moments later, I stepped out of the elevator on his floor.

I stalked into his office, and stopped short when I saw him talking to two men and with two children, both only six or seven, standing next to them. The boy and girl looked at me with wide eyes, and clung to one of the men's legs. Flickers of light danced around the other man, sparking with a subtle threat when he glanced at me.

Ronan grabbed his attention and shook his hand. "I promise, you'll all be safe. I'll be in touch in a few days, to check on you."

"Thank you," the protective sparking man said. "I don't know how we'll repay you."

"The debt is already paid. Safe travels." Ronan walked them to the door. The instant they were gone, as he turned to me, his eyes went cold and his expression blank.

"Good to see you, old friend." The greeting was the same as it had always been, but the warmth was gone from his voice.

I nodded. "And you."

"What can I do for you?"

I wouldn't be rude, but with Mia in an unknown condition, and waiting for me to return, I did need to make this conversation quick. I handed him the pill bottle. "What are these?"

"They look like a medication Mia takes." Ronan barely glanced at the bottle.

"She says you've had her take them since she was a child."

"I have. You've been spending a lot of time with her, haven't you?"

That hardly seemed relevant now. It was also an odd question, given Ronan told me she was in danger and asked me to keep her safe. "I have. And I'll continue to do so as long as she's threatened or as long as she wants me there."

"I see." Ronan gave a terse nod and turned away. "If she's missed a dose, you should get back to her."

Not without answers. "What do they treat? Why do they radiate Malsumis's energy?"

"I really think that's Mia's business, not yours." Ronan rested his weight on the edge of his desk, watching me with a piercing gaze.

This wasn't the friendship we shared. Nothing about this was right. Why was he being so evasive?

"I think that since they're imbued with a heavy magic, and she doesn't know what they're for, you should tell me," I said.

One moment Ronan's expression was cool, and the next frame he looked kind and sympathetic, like a bad movie special effect. "There's a good and terrifying reason that Mia is important to Kirby's cause," he said.

After the evasion and back and forth, we were going to launch into this new topic that was previously so taboo, he needed an isolated room to bring it up?

If I kept my thoughts to myself, would he talk us into answers without intending to?

"Mia has a dangerous magic embedded in her." A

faint convulsion ran through him, almost like an unformed gag. Before I could question it, the phony kindness was back.

"She doesn't think she has magic." So much for keeping my thoughts to myself.

Ronan shook his head. "She doesn't. Not that belongs to her, anyway. It's in her, but it's not hers. I don't know what it is or how to get it out, but the pills keep it squashed. They keep whatever it is from hurting those around her, and from destroying her."

"Like some sort of magical tumor?" I understood the explanation, but why keep it a secret from her? From me? From everyone.

"Exactly like that." As Ronan spoke, the air in the room changed. The energy around us shifted.

"Why keep it a secret?" If my questions were provoking this type of a response, I'd keep asking them aloud. It was almost as if a web was being woven from the ambient power in the air, and the individual lines sizzled as they pressed closer to me.

Why threaten me this way?

Why did Ronan still look like this was all normal? "Why didn't I tell Mia? For the same reason I kept anything from her—her safety."

"Why not tell me?" I extended my own pulse of energy to push back against the web. The threat loomed larger with each passing second, and the type of danger didn't make sense.

Ronan could take an entire building into a

different plane, but he was using parlor tricks. "Why would I give you such intimate information about my daughter?"

I swore there was emphasis on *intimate* and *my*. "Because you asked me to look out for her," said. "I can't do that if I don't know what I'm protecting her from."

"But I didn't need to ask you, did I? You've been far too attentive to her from the start. A child. *My* child." As Ronan spoke, the net of magic that he'd woven grew tighter. The threat was no longer subtle. "Tell me where she is, give me the pills, and I'll go get her. I never should've trusted you with her."

"She's an adult. She's capable of things like thinking for herself, and she belongs to no one but herself." I searched for a counter of my own, against Ronan's trap. "What happens if Mia stops taking the pills?"

"You don't want to find out. I'm not letting you go back to her."

The pressure squeezed me tightly now. Why did the conversation deteriorate this way? Was I even talking to Ronan? He'd done some stupid things in the time I'd known him, but this defied reason. "You never should've made these decisions on Mia's behalf."

"You don't actually believe that do you, old friend?" Ronan clucked.

I summoned a thread of electricity, highly localized lightning, to burn through the snare I was caught in, and destroyed the pills in my hand in the process. "I'm going back to Mia now. Without you. I hope you come to your senses before you seek her out."

"No. You're staying here." The threat in Ronan's voice was distinct.

I didn't care. I stalked to the exit, opened the door, and stepped into the same room.

Fuck. Ronan had enchanted the door so it was circular.

"Let me leave." I pushed the roll of thunder into my words.

"No."

Then I'd create my own exit. I reached deep and summoned the strength of the skies and the power of the storms. I coiled it all into a ball in my thoughts, winding tightly until the collection crackled and sparked in my mind.

I let the storm roll out in a shockwave that filled the air with ice and thunder. The wash froze the windows, and the pressure shattered them in a blink, sending shards of glass flying.

This was far more melodramatic an exit than I wanted to make, but Ronan had forced my hand. I walked to the window and jumped.

The dozens of story fall was cushioned by an invisible cloud of air cradling my feet, and I landed softly on the sidewalk.

Mia would've cheered for the superhero landed.

I needed to get back to her now. Get her somewhere safe, that didn't require a fae door to reach. Figure out where Caleb was…

And decide how to tell Mia her father wasn't the man she thought he was. Possibly literally, because I wasn't sure I'd just been talking to Ronan.

TWENTY
CALEB

My entire life, I'd wanted to know where I came from. Yes, I had loving, kind, generous parents, but the world they raised me in never felt like mine. I always thought it was because I was quirky, queer, and sarcastic. That I didn't fit in because some people just didn't, and I was one of those.

With all the changes recently, all the revelations about Mia, the demanding from Thac, the fact that I could set things on fire with my own fucking hands…

That made the need to know who I was even more intense.

And now I was standing in this new place that felt like I belonged here, like I was always meant to be here. I was looking at a woman who was so familiar it ached, and she was promising me answers. I wanted this to be my reality more than anything.

More than *almost* anything.

Mia wasn't here—she was in a house on a beach feeling ill, and as soon as she was better, I wanted to dance and watch bad movies and roll around naked in the sand with her.

Thac wasn't here—he was looking after her, instead of having my back here. Instead of pushing me. Opening my eyes. Tempting me with magic and thoughts that made me wonder what it would be like to throw myself at him when I wasn't all but drunk.

But I was here, and here felt right too. I hoped. "Who are you?" I asked. "Can you give me answers?"

"I'm Artura, and I'll try. Would you like to sit? I would've made coffee and cookies, but I didn't know you were coming. I didn't know…" She trailed off with a frown and gestured to the chairs around the kitchen table. "Sit."

I did, because no matter how odd this situation was, it felt more normal than day to day life. It was day to day life, except that I'd been magically teleported here. "I don't need coffee. Trust me, the last thing I need is to be more wired. I do need…" What? Where was I supposed to start? "Who are you? Who am I?"

She took the seat across from me. Physically she looked younger than me, but her eyes held eons of knowledge, and I wanted to glean it all. "Once upon a time, not too long ago in fact, I gave someone a lot like you some very vague answers in response to those questions. I'd been doing so for so long, being cryptic and trying to lead people to their own conclusions, that it made sense to keep doing so."

"No offense, but this still sounds like a vague, cryptic answer."

One corner of her mouth tugged up. "I suppose it does. My name varies depending on the culture and the period. For the longest time, I was known as Verdandy. I currently prefer Artura. I'm one of three dragons who came into existence before humanity. Before gods. Before anyone."

It was a beautiful tale. It had kind of a Brothers Grimm feel to it, or maybe something more biblical. It wasn't much more than Thac had given me. "Are you my mother?" It should've been a ridiculous question to ask of a stranger.

"Yes." Her answer, simple and direct, sent a wave of emotion through me so potent I gasped on the feelings.

It was impossible to sift through them or identify any of them, so I let them permeate me instead. "How… I don't… Why did you leave me?"

Artura wrung her hands, then stood and paced into the kitchen. She grabbed an intricate porcelain jar from a cabinet and set it down. Her entire frame shook as she stood with her back to me, and her hands pressed into a tile countertop. "I thought you were dead. So many years ago, I watched you bur— You were supposed to be a dragon. Fire shouldn't have hurt you. You were supposed to be…" She faced me again. "And maybe you still are. You're here after all."

"I've been living in upstate New York." Sitting didn't feel right. I crossed the room to join her, took the coffee she'd just pulled out, and set up the French press to brew. I was going to be wired regardless, so I might as well enjoy the brew. "I was adopted as a baby."

I shouldn't have been able to find any of it without asking, but it was all where I would've put it, if this was my house. I opened a cupboard or a drawer and there was each next item I needed. "I only found out a few days ago that magic was a thing. That there was more than one god. That I could do things I never thought were real." I held out my hand and let it grow and shift into a series of claws and gnarled fingers.

"You have control." Artura sounded amazed.

Control over what? "*Am* I a dragon? Thac said there were only three. What's going on?" It seemed the more answers I got, the more I needed.

Artura grabbed a jar that was shaped like a cat, one of those lucky cats from Japan. She opened it and started arranging cookies from inside on a serving tray. Little biscuit sandwich cookies.

This entire scene was so serene and domestic, and I was talking to a creature who claimed to be hundreds of thousands—millions—of years old. How did someone stay sane for that long? Thac said he'd stopped counting after a thousand years.

"I'll start at the beginning. It will seem tedious, but everything will make more sense that way. You can ask any questions and I will try to answer them directly if I can." Artura poured two cups of coffee and set them next to the tray. The entire arrangement vanished from the counter and reappeared on the kitchen table. Could I do that?

I joined her at the table again. "I've always loved a good story."

She smiled. "Wait until you see the bookstore downstairs." She sipped her coffee black and nibbled on one of the sandwich cookies.

I wanted to interrupt with *you own a fucking bookstore*? It wasn't the most important thing I could ask about, not by far, but it made this entire thing seem both more real and more surreal at the same time. Instead, I enjoyed my own cookie and waited for her to tell the story.

"Millennia ago, there were three sisters," Artura said. "We existed on stories and each other's company, and the tales we told each other were glorious. Sweeping epics about beings we'd never seen before, though later we'd call them things like human. They made smart decisions and stupid decisions and they fell in love and they fell in hate. They warred. They fucked. They made more of themselves.

"Imagine your favorite book or TV show, where

you're rooting for a character or hoping for their demise or feeling any other number of emotions in between. Those were what our stories were to us. We had our favorites and our least favorites. We told the same tales again and again, adding new details each time. We didn't know where these glorious images came from, but we all saw them, as plain as day, in our heads."

Artura's gaze fell on her plate, and she stared, her gaze reaching past anything in this room, to a time I had trouble imagining.

Should I say something? Was she lost in the thought? Was she coming back?

She blinked several times fast and took another drink. "The first time we met creatures like we'd imagined, we were stunned. The first time something happened to them that was identical to the stories we'd told, we didn't understand. How could they know? How could we have known?

"Over time, we saw more and more of the things happen to them that we'd told each other stories about. We realized as dozens and hundreds of seasons passed, that we'd been seeing their lives play out before any of it ever happened. Sometimes we tried to stop the bad from happening to our favorites. Sometimes we tried to make it happen to those we hadn't liked. It never mattered. Things played out exactly the way we'd seen them, over and over."

I should be having the hardest time wrapping my

brain around all of this. Like when Thac told me he was a god, I should be staring at Artura and wondering if I should call the men in white coats. But it all sounded real and plausible. "So… what? You were prophets?"

Her laugh was raucous and bitter and ended in a snap of her jaw. "We've been called fates, meddlers, most cursed ones, and yes, prophets. We were originally just sisters telling each other stories we thought were a product of our imagination."

"And after all this time, millennia, *now* was when you decided to have a child?" It might not have been the most important part of the story to focus on, but it was what I could wrap my head around, while I tried to grasp the rest of this vast picture.

Artura—my mother—shook her head. "We've had children with mortals, immortals, and gods for as long as we've known them. For the most part, our offspring take on the traits of their other parent. There are surges in time where our children are born with the ability to become dragons instead."

"So there are others out there like me." Or did they all grow up knowing where they came from? "Thac said there were only three of you."

Sadness rushed from Artura, and then the sensation vanished as if it had never been there. "Those who were born in the past are gone. Until very recently, there were only three of us again. Yes, there are others like you now. One of the visions my sisters and I had when we were very young was of a strange place none of us could describe. None of the world we saw made sense. Looking back, it's easy to see that it was now, but in a world of nothing but stone and water and simple plants, things like printed books and cars and computers were something we shouldn't have been able to imagine.

"The vision we shared, the story, was about our children. Our sons. Our daughters. Each of you is so different and unique and headstrong." This time her grief lingered, splashed across her face and painted in the creases on her forehead. "I was certain it was wrong, because thirty years ago I watched you both die. Skuld must've taken you. Hidden you… How did I not know? How did I not see?"

Wait. What did she say? "Both?"

The doorknob on the apartment rattled and I spun in my seat to look. A woman stepped into the room, and her smirk when her gaze fell on me made my blood run cold. "You found us."

I knew her. She was the woman I met in the church. But that wasn't possible, because this woman looked different. She was almost like looking in a mirror, except that her eyeliner was more on point than mine had ever been.

"Yes, both," Artura said. "Caleb, this is your twin sister, Callie."

TWENTY-ONE
MIA

I WAS ALMOST CERTAIN THAT WHEN WE GOT HERE, THE house had been decorated in subtle earth tones. Browns. Beiges. A splash of evergreen here and there, and maybe some hints of gold and navy.

As I looked around now at Thac's room, the colors were all…

Colorful.

My first thought was *wrong,* but it was all so right instead. It wasn't like rainbows or prisms or double vision. I wasn't hallucinating. Probably. It was just that everything around me was more vibrant and rich. It radiated with extra layers. The entire room had more depth.

That sounded weird, even in my own head. I pressed my hand to my forehead and lay back on the bed to stare at the ceiling.

The wood above me ran in neat slats, but I could

pick out individual knots in each board. The imperfections. The stunning, fluid flaws that made the entire thing real and organic, rather than mass manufactured.

Maybe it was a good thing Thac left me here. Being alone with my thoughts did the opposite of keeping me from worrying about Caleb, though. And why wasn't Thac back yet?

My entire childhood, the reminder was always there to take the pills. It was one of the few habits I'd formed and stuck to. Those rare occasions I forgot for half a day, the dizziness reminded me before things got bad. Was this a repercussion of letting the…

What was wrong with me?

Thac asked what the pills were for.

I needed them. The thought rushed in ahead of all the others. It wasn't what I wanted to be thinking though. What did I have? Some sort of syndrome? Condition? Disease?

I needed the pills. Now. I needed them before bad things happened.

What things? Why did it feel like half of these thoughts weren't my own?

"Hello?" A familiar voice carried through the house.

Astrid?

Now I was really hallucinating.

"Mia." That was Magnus's sharp call. Without question.

Was I about to be talking to the voices in my head? "In here," I replied with trepidation.

A moment later, Magnus and Astrid stepped into view. "*Here* is not a location," Magnus said.

"Did you expect her to send you map coordinates? Latitude and longitude would've been more helpful?" Astrid joined me, studying me.

Magnus shrugged and hung back, keeping her attention outside the room. "Something more helpful than *here* would've been good."

"I didn't know if you were real, or where you were." If I was talking to my imagination, at least it was appropriately snarky. "Would *master bedroom* have been more helpful? It's not a big house." I poked Astrid in the leg. "You feel real."

Astrid knelt on the floor next to me. "We're real. Are you all right?" Her tone was kind. Concerned. "Why would you be imagining us?"

An ache throbbed behind my eye, and what felt like a cracking sensation spread along my scalp. "I don't know." Where was Thac? "Why are you here?"

Astrid furrowed her brow and studied me. "You look different." She turned her head away and glanced at me out of the corner of her eye. "Why do you look different?"

"Dahlia saw something," Magnus said from her position. "Her visions of the future are sometimes only a few seconds or minutes off. She said you needed help, and it felt urgent. We would've been here sooner, but there was something blocking us from getting in."

The wards Thac put up. "How did you get past them?" I asked.

"Magnus can break some wards." Astrid reached for me. She grasped my wrist, but pulled away with a shudder, like she'd just touched something unpleasant. "You said you weren't magic."

"I'm not. Turns out my father is an elf though. Fae? Whatever. It didn't pass on to me." I shouldn't be telling them this, but I trusted these women. I had from the moment I met them, even if I hadn't recognized it.

Magnus looked reluctant to leave her post, but joined us at the bed. She studied me. "Yeah, you're right. I see something. It's more like a wall than a shield." She glided the hand with the claw ring along my skin, never making contact. Heat flowed between us regardless.

A crackling sounded in my ears, and the hair stood up on the back of my neck. It was like being buzzed by a sock fresh out of the dryer. The longer she moved, the more my discomfort grew.

Sharp shocks crackled over me, and I yelped and jerked away. "What was that?"

"A much stronger blocker than it looks like." Astrid was studying me again. "I think someone has blocked your magic."

That was a thing? "Why? How can you tell?"

"Because my mother did it to me," Astrid said. "As for the why, I can't say. It's a horrible thing to do to someone. Looking at you, it's almost as if you're covered with a fractured shell of yourself, and the cracks show the magic starting to show through."

I didn't understand. I had magic? I couldn't… I didn't…

"We need to fix you." Astrid knitted her brows. "This is making you sick."

And yet, I was focused on the fact that Thac was going to be upset to come home to all these strangers in his house. Why wasn't he back? "How do we do that?"

"I don't know." Astrid turned to Magnus. "Spread out. Look for anything that might help? Plants that are magic. Traces of magic somewhere else. There has to be something we can use to help her."

None of this was right, and the nagging feeling in my gut that I needed to be doing something besides laying here and fucking around, was growing stronger with each passing moment.

TWENTY-TWO
CALEB

I WANTED TO BE CONFUSED BY THESE MOST RECENT events. Given everything I'd seen in the last few days alone, this was a drop in the bucket.

It was like Mia had said before, this all felt right. It all made sense. This was a truth that I felt in my gut—I was talking to my mother and my sister.

Yet, for as long as I'd wanted to know where I came from, and who my birth parents were, I couldn't stay here. "I am so happy I found you both, and I want to know everything about you. About who we are and who I am. Unfortunately, I was in the middle of something."

"You need to learn who you are and how to control the gift you have." Artura's tone left no room for argument.

I was going to argue anyway. "Are you going to teach me all of that in a day? In an hour?"

"I assume this will take months to become familiar with the basics, and years to perfect," she said.

Who could put their life on hold for that long? Magic or not, I still had to go back to something when this was all over. If so few knew dragons were real, and even fewer knew there were more than a couple, I didn't expect it was the kind of thing that would get me a better job or life once I'd learned how to be one.

I had other questions, too. "Why didn't you come for me? How did you not know I was alive?"

"I saw you die." A hint of emotion slipped into Artura's reply.

I looked at Callie—why was she so quiet? She didn't so much as flinch, though she obviously knew about both Artura and me before now.

"You wouldn't be a prisoner or confined here in any way," Artura said. "You can come and go, but I'd like this to be your home. I'd like to get to know my child, and help you learn."

"I want that too." More than I'd ever realized. Yes, I had a mother who had raised me, and whom I loved. I'd wanted this feeling for as long as I could remember though—to know where I belonged.

I had that with Mia. The realization was impossible to ignore. She felt like coming home. There was even a little of that with Thac. But Artura made me feel like that too.

"I know this is a lot to process." Callie finally spoke. "I've been dealing with it months longer than you, and I'm just wrapping my head around it. Do you want to walk with me? Find a cafe and talk and process?"

What I wanted was to get back to Mia. The pull was strong. That feeling that she wasn't doing well. This wasn't the time to drag my feet and be indecisive, but acting without enough information could be dangerous. If Callie could give me that from the perspective of someone who had recently lived what I was going through…

"I've been here longer than humanity," Artura said. "I want to get to know my son, but my existence has taught me there are few things that can't wait a few hours or even a few years. I'll be here when you get back."

I needed answers and to stop feeling like I was always one step behind. "All right," I said to Callie.

We headed down a staircase that seemed to run behind a shop. When we stepped outside, we were in a back alley. A large mural ran up the multi-story brick wall, of shelves of books with a dragon wrapped around them.

Neat. On the nose, but really cool.

We stepped onto the main street, and I was greeted by stone buildings that were too close together, and streets that were too narrow for the small cars that drove on them.

"Where are we?" Another question. At least this one should have an answer.

Callie picked a direction with purpose, as if she knew exactly where we were going. "Spain."

Oh. So, Artura had teleported us across the world without one of those nifty fairy gates. "Can you and I teleport too?"

"Yes," Callie said. "We can also see visions of the future, look like anyone, and summon fire."

I'd gotten the summon fire part, but the rest… Maybe being a dragon wasn't too bad.

"There's a little place down the street with espresso and pastries." She gestured.

I couldn't visit a new-to-me country and not at least try the food. "Sounds good. Why didn't you tell Artura you knew I was alive? You sought me out. You knew who I was."

Callie watched her feet as we walked. "It'll help if you have a little backstory. There were only three dragons until recently, and then one died."

That sounded like what Thac said, except for the last bit.

"They got around—the dragons. They used their ability to change their appearance to be whatever gender they felt like at the time, and have whatever features they wanted. In other words, there have been a lot of little dragon babies throughout time."

Made sense. Ancient beings fucking a lot. That was one of the most logical parts of all of this so far. "But none of them were actually dragons, if there have only been three before now."

"No." Callie shook her head. "As I understand it, there are these moments in time, spots in history, where a generation of those children become dragons. Not all of them, but more than a couple. Supposedly it's super rare, as in it's only ever happened a couple of times. Both of those times, they all died except the three."

That was horrific. "And it's happening again." How did they die? How would we die? Was she saying it happened because they changed, or did they still live normal lives and just not become immortal? Something in between? How was this conversation making more questions than it answered?

"Basically, yes. None of us know who we are before the change starts to happen, but at least most of them have someone around who's familiar with magic. Has some sort of idea of what might be happening to them." Bitterness slunk into her voice.

I wouldn't have called having Thac there when I first did something big a *good thing* but was it better than going through it alone? Probably. "What about you?"

"I was alone. I'd spent the day teaching—I used to be a professor at an ivy league school—and was in my office after a long day. The first change was fire, and it was terrifying. I blacked out for a few minutes, and when I woke up, I'd set everything around me on fire. I lost years of research."

"I'm so sorry." I could only imagine how much that would hurt.

Her laugh was a bark. "Not that it mattered. My research was about a series of ancient texts that I found, that I've since learned were prophecies by our mother and her sisters. I was interpreting them wrong. Have you had the visions yet? Have you seen things in the future that terrify you and are incredibly threatening?"

That didn't sound pleasant. "No."

We'd reached the coffee shop and paused the conversation long enough to take a seat and give our orders to the waiter.

When he was gone, Callie let out a shaky sigh. "Yeah, so I burned down my office, I was charged with arson. Fired for it. My fiancé left me. My chance for tenure, or to ever teach anywhere else of note is gone. I wanted to care, but I had to let it fall apart because the shift to becoming a dragon, the pain, the confusion, took too much of my attention to let me focus on the important things."

I couldn't imagine. It had sucked for me to change in front of Thac, but at least it meant he was there to give me *some* insight. To tell me I wasn't going insane, I was just magic. Even if he wasn't the kindest about it, he also could've been more cruel. Or I could've gone through the whole thing alone. "How did you find your way here?"

"A god came to me one night. He'd sought me out

and he had answers. Understanding. A copy of my research with notes about where I needed to adjust my thinking." She snorted. "Yeah, I was still worried about that."

"Which god?"

"Does it matter?"

I didn't suppose so, except that her instant evasion of the question was odd. "I kind of feel like it does."

"How much control do you have? It's my understanding that most of us have a hard time with what happens at first."

I showed her the clawed hand, careful not to be flashy about the display in front of other patrons. "I don't know. There was one accidental fire, but I have no clue what I can and can't do." Aside from the list I'd been given. I did want to try all of that. "You have control, because you looked like someone else in the church."

"I learned. I was taught. None of that is anything you want to go through if you don't have to." She sounded haunted.

It made sense there were methods other than those Thac had tried, but I wasn't sure I wanted to think about it. "What gives you—us—control?"

"Admitting we're not human. Surrendering the part of ourselves that clings to our mortality."

In some ways, I'd done that a long time ago.

A series of images flashed in my mind, there and gone so quickly I couldn't grasp them. I frowned.

"Are you all right?" Callie asked.

I shook off the strange sensation. "I'm fine. You shouldn't have had to go through that alone."

"No kidding. But I have what I need now, and you'll be a lot happier if you stay and learn from Mom than if anyone else teaches you."

It was odd that she called Artura *Mom* so easily. Though it also seemed weird to me that I swore I could feel Callie's pain. "I have a life. People who need me," I said.

"We need you. I promise you, everyone in your life will abandon you when they find out what you really are, including the immortals who said they'd help. Including the Valkyrie."

My frown was back. What Valkyrie? Instinct said she was talking about Mia, who I hadn't mentioned. How did Callie know about her, but not that Mia wasn't a Valkyrie?

More images flashed in my mind, like watching a video, it was a third person view of the fight outside of Ronan's building. When a not-Valkyrie had attacked us. I'd see the shape of a dragon in the blur, and in my thoughts, it was clear now. It was vivid.

It was Callie.

I stared at her. This wasn't a thought she needed to hear.

Her emotion faded and she raised an eyebrow. "We're tied to them, to the Valkyries. I don't know how or why, but one of them gets their wings and one of us awakens."

Our coffee arrived, putting an awkward pause on the intensity of the moment. The brief respite gave me a chance to grasp for my thoughts as I picked at my pastry. Bits of this were terrifying, and others felt too easy. Some of these answers were so…

Convenient.

"I don't know any new Valkyries. Not that I'm aware of." That was a truth on my part, even if it left out details of what I knew about Mia. Was Callie feeding me information in the same way?

"I don't either," she said. "Or rather, I didn't. When the woman I'm tied to was given her powers, I wasn't there. I had no idea who she was. It still impacted me."

Did that mean I was tied to someone besides Mia? The thought was sour in my head and my gut, but it must be true because she hadn't become—

My mind sidestepped into a new series of images. A video. A man I'd seen twice in Mia's comic shop. The man she said was Odin, talking to Callie.

I couldn't stop my gaze from drifting to her.

"Are you all right?" Her voice was guarded.

I shook my head. "Good coffee." Why was she lying to me? Some of her story was true, I felt that, but which parts and how much?

"Will you stay? Learn with me?" Callie hadn't touched her drink or food.

I wanted to know more about everything, but there had to be a balance. "I'm not going to move to Spain or anything. I have to check on Mia. I have a life. I'll come for regular lessons."

"I'm tired of doing this alone. I don't... We finally belong. How do you not want to embrace that?"

"I do want to." Come with me. Met Mia. Meet Thac. The offer was on the tip of my tongue, but something held me back from making it.

The video was back in my head, but this time it was a man I'd only seen in pictures. He had Mia's eyes—or she had his—and there was a photo on his desk of someone who looked a lot like Mia, but paler. More gaunt. I'd seen that picture too.

I was seeing Ronan, moving in an office that looked like it was made of woodlands. Talking to Odin and Callie.

Her voice was distant, calling my name, but I was stuck in the movie that played out in front of me. I had no choice but to watch this unfold as Ronan argued with Odin. As the two men went back and forth about Ragnarök and gods and power and prophecies.

Callie watched it all, somehow looking as imposing as Thac ever had despite her smaller stature.

Odin touched his fingers to Ronan's face. "You will do this my way, one way or another. Even if I have to force you."

He was mind controlling Ronan.

I had no idea where the thought came from, but I was certain it was real.

Odin and Callie walked out of the office, and Ronan grabbed his phone. A moment later he said, "Evening. I'm sorry to call during your downtime, I need you here, though."

The vision vanished and I was back in the coffee shop. The abrupt change in scenery jarred my brain. What had I seen?

Not the future. What I was watching had already happened. Instinct said so.

I focused on Callie again, who was watching me with a strange combination of curiosity and hesitation.

"What did you see?" she asked.

"Why?" Not exactly the most helpful answer on my part, but it wasn't like she'd given me the truth.

"You look the way we look when we're having a vision. Yours was almost peaceful though. More like when Mom falls into the future."

What I saw wasn't peaceful, despite the lack of physical violence. And it wasn't the future. "Why are you working with Odin?"

Her smile turned darker. "I told you. He saved me. He came to me when no one else was there."

"And you watched as he cast some sort of mind control on Ronan."

"How did you—" She twisted her mouth. "I

planned to tell you myself, when I knew you'd understand. What did you see?"

"It doesn't matter. I need to get home." I pushed back from the table. How did I summon the power to take me back to Thac's bungalow?

Callie rose as well and grasped my arm. "I'm sorry but you can't, Brother. You need to come with me."

An intense weakness washed through me, and the cafe vanished. We were in a room that looked both like it went on forever, and that it stopped a few feet from my face.

"I'll explain," she said. "But you need to stay here while I do so."

"So good to finally meet you." A new voice came from behind me, and I turned to see Odin standing with us.

TWENTY-THREE
MIA

I WAS MAGIC. I *HAD* MAGIC.

It was tucked away under a shell that was cracking.

Was that my father's doing? Why would he…? He'd lied to me about who we were, but would he really hide this from me? The fact that I was more? Knowing my entire life how badly I wanted something like this, and he'd not only kept its existence from me, but kept my own abilities tucked away?

Maybe I was more like the X-men than I thought.

I wanted to help Magnus and Astrid search the property for a solution, but even with powers, I was stuck in bed, dizzy. Not that I would have any idea what to be searching for.

Dear me, suck it up and stop being a baby about this. The stern command rocked in my skull.

It was a good point. I couldn't just sit here and do nothing. I had to act. I had to—

"I might have something," Magnus called, and walked back into the room.

Astrid rejoined us as well. "Good, because I got nothin'."

"Is that mistletoe?" I stared at the long, slender leaves and white berries in Magnus's hand.

Magnus nodded. "I can't see anything else, but legend says this is what killed Baldur."

"That seems like the kind of thing I wouldn't want to take." Wait. A plant killed a god? "Or even be around." Why did Thac have such a dangerous thing growing near his house? Did he know? Was he safe here?

"No, I think she's onto something." Astrid took the berries from Magnus. "In the ancient past, we used these in potions and concoctions due to the belief of its anti-magical properties. The results varied, and most of them could have been because of the poisonous nature of the plant, but I'm more certain now there was some truth to the belief. If your power is being blocked by a stronger power, this could break it."

The logic made sense, but only to a point. "What if it kills my native magic, too? Or me."

Astrid tilted her head and raked her gaze over me. "You're so much more powerful than you realize. It's why this is starting to crack. Your strength is forcing its way through. I have no idea how the block on you lasted so many years, but the mistletoe won't kill you or your magic."

No. I was no one. I was weak, giant Mia, and I hated myself for it.

Except, I wasn't.

"You need to do something," Astrid said. "This is tearing you down in bad ways. We can start small. A tiny dose, just to see if it helps weaken the block, but not enough to permanently hurt what's a part of you. I promise, the last thing I want is to hurt you."

Should I—

A new force rushed through me. Terror. Pain. Rage.

"Something's wrong with Caleb." I didn't mean to say that aloud. "And Thac."

"Caleb?" Magnus asked.

"He's my roommate. And a dragon, apparently."

Astrid and Magnus exchanged a look.

I really didn't like that.

"Like a dragon you feel an intense pull to?"

I wouldn't have described it that way, but now that Magnus mentioned it… "I guess so."

"We need to make you better so we can find him," Astrid said.

Yes. That was the best suggestion yet. Caleb was in trouble. We had to get to him. Now. I needed to…

The room spun and the strength sapped from me.

"Making tea. Now." Astrid hurried from the room.

A few minutes later, she was back with a delicate cup that had steam rising above the lip. She handed it to me. "Very small dose. It'll probably taste like grass."

"Mmm… Yummy." I let out a long breath, and swallowed several gulps.

She was right—it tasted like watery grass. At least it wasn't revolting, even though it would never make my list of *I'd try this again willingly*.

"What are you doing here?" Thac's sharp question jarred my attention away from the cup. He was standing near the closet door, having just stepped into to the room.

"They're here to help me." My voice sounded weird to my ears. Hollow. Echoey. "They're friends. They're—"

Light exploded behind my eyelids, accompanied by rage. Agony.

Something bad was happening to Caleb.

Whatever was going on with me wasn't great either. It felt like a million tiny fractures ran along my skin. No, this wasn't a bad feeling. It was like the thin chocolate shell on an ice cream sundae cracking. But I was the ice cream. I was starting to melt without the shell to hold me together.

My shoulder blades felt itchy. Wrong.

No. This was a good feeling. This was right.

My head was clearing, leaving the screaming

alarm that said Caleb needed us. I looked up to find Thac, Astrid, and Magnus staring at me.

"Those aren't Valkyrie wings," Magnus said.

Wings? What? Where?

Astrid shook her head. "No. They're not."

"They're fae wings." Thac was staring at me as though he was seeing me for the first time.

What? I had what? I caught a glimpse of myself in the full-length mirror behind Thac, and my reflection captured my gaze. Lithe, translucent wings spread from my back. The gossamer texture reflected colors I'd never seen before.

The warning bells in my head screamed louder, demanding I give the feeling attention. Caleb was hurt. Badly.

For Astrid's story, and to read another book in the Valkyries Rising series, check out VALKYRIE RENEWED. The world needs saving and Astrid's Magic can help. Too bad she has no memory of this power.

- Click here to start reading VALKYRIE RENEWED
- Check out the next page in this book for the other authors and books in the Valkyrie Rising series

---

If you haven't read Dahlia's story yet, make sure to check out the NEON series, starting with SUBVERSION. TOM isn't willing to let a valuable resource like Dahlia slip away. Rather than try to hide, Frey's going to stick her in the spotlight, headlining as the club's newest burlesque star, so she knows where her enemies are looking for her. But there are dangers the three haven't accounted for, including surrendering their hearts.

- Secure your copy of SUBVERSION today

OTHER VALKYRIES RISING BOOKS

VALKYRIE DESTINED by Allyson Lindt

Azzie, Zeke, and Davyn

She was raised on the prophecies that defined her future, but when the reality of destiny comes to light, she's not prepared for the consequences.

VALKYRIE LOST by Shannon Pemrick

Astrid and Tyr

As the god of war and bringer of order and justice he can have anything. Except one mortal woman. (This is a prequel to Shannon Pemrick's books about Astrid and her men, and takes place in the past)

VALKYRIE RENEWED by Shannon Pemrick

Astrid, Tyr, and Diego

The world needs saving and Astrid's Magic can help. Too bad she has no memory of this power.

VALKYRIE RESTORED by TB Mann

Elin, Arran, and Hurrit

Memory loss can be a blessing or a curse... She just hasn't decided which.

VALKYRIE CONFUSED by Sotia Lazu

Scarlett, Pan, and Arnlaug

Berserkers? Gods? Valkyries? Are they real, or a fantasy wild enough to be in her next book?

www.ingramcontent.com/pod-product-compliance
Lightning Source LLC
LaVergne TN
LVHW091036080826
845145LV00002B/521

* 9 7 8 1 9 5 5 5 1 8 6 9 7 *